# WHEN THE ATOMS FAILED

By
JOHN W. CAMPBELL, JR.

ARMCHAIR FICTION
PO Box 4369, Medford, Oregon 97504

*The original text of this edition was first published by Experimenter Publications, Inc.*

Armchair Edition, Copyright 2016 by Gregory J. Luce
All Rights Reserved

*For more information about Armchair Books and products, visit our website at...*

**www.armchairfiction.com**

*Or email us at...*

**armchairfiction@yahoo.com**

# Part One:
## *When the Atoms Failed*

### FOREWORD TO PART ONE

WHEN the events of which I am to tell took place all the world was interested solely in their final outcome, but when that last awful day was ended, and time enough had passed to give our world a chance to find a way to apply and use the awful forces it had had forced upon it, or, indeed had even found how to control their immense energies, men began to wonder about the true story of the Invasion.

I had always been a writer, first newspaper work, then a book or two. Perhaps because of this the world expected that an account would soon be presented. But had those millions seen that awful battle, seen those mighty wrecks on the hot sands, even then might they understand my dread of telling of that titanic conflict—a conflict in which the weaker was a million times more powerful than any force man had previously seen! It still burns in my memory, that awful scene in its desolate setting—the vast rolling desert below, seared, bladed, fused in great streaks where the intense, stabbing heat rays had cut it, mighty craters blasted in its surface where the terrific explosions of the shells had heaved thousands of tons of sand into great mounds, and those ghastly wrecks that lay crushed and broken on the hot sands below, bathed in the ruddy light of the sun of sunset, now slowly sinking behind the distant purple hills, as the last of the Invaders crashed on the packed sands below.

Two men of all Earth's billions saw that scene—but those two will never forget—as Stephen Waterson and I can testify.

Ten years have passed, ten years of stupendous change, readjustment, and cosmic conquest. Ten years in which a world has been added to man's domain, yet still sharp and clear in my memory is the picture of those shapeless masses, those lumps of glowing metal, that lay on the sands beneath us, the sole vestiges of the mighty ships of Mars.

Never have I wanted to think long on that scene of titanic destruction, destruction such as man never before knew, but friends have convinced me that it is my duty as one who lived in closest contact with the facts, and one of the two men who saw that last struggle, to tell the story as it unrolled itself before me.

Brief it is. The entire event, for all its consequences, lasted but two days—days that changed the history of a Universe!

But in this march of mighty events, I was but a spectator, and as a spectator I shall tell it. And I shall try to depict for you the character of the greatest man of all the System's history—Stephen Waterson.

Waterson Laboratories
May, 1957
David Gale.

# CHAPTER ONE

IT was late afternoon in May, 1947, and the temperature had climbed to unbelievable heights during the day. It seemed impossible to work with that merciless sun beating down on the roof. It is odd that a temperature of 95 in May should seem far higher than a similar temperature in July. On the top floors of the great apartments it was stifling. The great disadvantage of roof landings for planes had always been the tendency of the roofs to absorb heat in summer, yet on the topmost floors of those apartments people were living, and in one of those apartments a man was trying to work. Heat was a great trouble, but he found thoughts of hunger in the not too distant future an even greater inspiration to work. The manuscript he was correcting was lengthy, but this was the final revision, which was some comfort. Still the low buzz of the telephone annunciator was a relief. It was so much easier to talk. He took up the telephone.

"Gale speaking."

"Hello Dave, this is Steve. I hear you are having a bit of hot weather in New York today. I have a suggestion for you—I'm coming to pick you up in an hour and a half, and if you will be ready on your roof then, in a camp suit, and with camp clothes for about a month packed, I can guarantee you some fun, providing of course that you're still the man I knew. But I can't guarantee to return you! Meet me on your roof in an hour and a half."

"Well, I'll—now what's up?" The receiver on the other end clicked. "So he isn't sure I'll get back—and he calls that a 'suggestion'! Anyhow it sounds interesting and I'll have to hurry. I wish he'd get into the habit of warning a fellow when he is going to start one of his expeditions! And I may not come back—I wonder where on Earth he's going now—and where he was then. The only reason he gives me an hour and a half is because it will take him that long to get here. He would drop in on me without any notice otherwise. In that case he must be about three hundred miles from here. But where?"

AN hour and a half later he was on the roof, watching the darting planes, there were a good many, but by far the larger part of the world's business and pleasure was on the ground in those days. Still the crimson and gray special of Waterson's ought to be easily visible. He was late—unusual for Steve. Gale hadn't seen him in more than a year—probably been working on one of his eternal experiments, he decided.

Still he searched the skies in vain. Only the regular planes, and one dirigible—tiny in the distance—it seemed to be coming toward him—and it certainly was coming rapidly—it couldn't be a dirigible—no gas bag could go that fast—then he saw the crimson and the gray band around it—it was Steve.

And now as it darted down and landed gracefully on the roof beside him, he saw that the machine was but thirty-five feet long, and ten or so in diameter. Suddenly a small round hatchway opened in its curved, windowless side of polished metal, and a moment later Stephen Waterson forced his way out. The door was certainly small, and forcing that six-foot-two body in and out through it must have been a feat worthy of a magician. Gale noticed that he would just about fit it, but the giant Waterson must have intended to use it very infrequently to make it that size.

"Hello, Dave—how do you like my new boat? But get in, we're going. There, your bag's in already."

"Good Lord, Steve, what is this? I gather you invented it. Certainly I never saw nor heard of it before," said Gale.

"Well Dave, I suppose you might say I invented it, but the truth is that a machine invented it—or at least discovered the principles on which it is based."

"A machine! A machine invented it? What do you mean? A machine can't think, can it?"

"I'm not so sure they can't, Dave, but get in—I'll tell you later. I promised Wright I would be back in three hours, and I've lost ten minutes already. Also, this machine weighs three thousand tons—so I don't want to leave it on this roof longer than is absolutely necessary."

"But, Steve—let me look at it. Man, it is beautiful. What is that metal?"

"Try the inside, Dave—there!"

Dave Gale was rather good sized—five feet ten, and weighing over one hundred and sixty pounds, but Waterson was in perfect physical condition, two hundred and ten pounds of solid muscle, and Gale had been popped into the hatch like a bag of meal, so quickly was it done.

Now he turned to look at the tiny room in which he found himself. It was evidently the pilot room, and around the front of the room there ran a clear window, curved to fit the curve of the ship's walls, and about three feet high, the center coming at about the level of the eye of a person sitting in either of the two deeply cushioned chairs directly facing it. The chairs were evidently an integral part of the machine, and from the heavy straps attached to them it was obvious that the passengers were expected to need some support. The arms of each chair were fully two feet broad, and many small instruments and controls were arranged on their polished black surfaces. Waterson had seated himself in the right hand chair and strapped himself in. Gale hastened to secure himself in the left chair.

"Take it easy Dave, and be prepared for a shock when we start."

"I'm ready Steve, let's go!"

Waterson moved his right hand a bit, and a tiny red bulb showed on his left instrument panel; many of his instruments began to give readings and several on Gale's board did so also. Another movement, and there was a muffled hum of an air blower. Then Waterson looked at Gale and turned a small venier dial—Gale had been watching intently—but suddenly the look left his face—and was replaced by a look of astonished pain. The entire car had suddenly jerked a bit, then that peculiarly unpleasant sensation connected most intimately with a rapid elevator or helicopter starting from rest had made itself unpleasantly pronounced. Gale's pained and somewhat sick expression caused Waterson's smile to broaden.

"Whew—Steve—what is this—why don't you warn a fellow of what's coming!"

"I did warn you, Dave," answered Waterson, "and if you will look out, I think you will understand this."

THE car was rising, at first slowly, but ever faster and faster, from the roof, not as a helicopter rises, not as a dirigible rises, but more as a heavy body falls, with high acceleration ever faster and faster. Soon it was rising quite rapidly, straight up. Then another tiny red bulb flashed into life on Waterson's switchboard, and the ship suddenly tilted at an angle of thirty degrees. Then it shot forward, and continually accelerated an already great speed, till New York lay far behind, and then the sky became dark and black, and now the stars were looking in at them, not the winking, blue stars of Earth, but the blazing, steady stars of infinite space, and they were of every color, dull reds, greenish, and blue. And now as they shot on across the face of Earth far below,

Gale watched in rapture the magnificent view before him, seeking the old friends of Earth—Mars, Venus, Jupiter, and the other familiar, gleaming points. Then he turned his gaze toward the Sun, and cried out in astonishment, for the giant sphere was a hard, electric blue, like some monster electric arc, and for millions of miles there swept from it a great hazy, glowing cloud, the zodiacal light, almost invisible from Earth, but here blazing out in indescribable beauty.

"We're in space! But, Steve, look at the sun! What makes it look blue? The glass of the window isn't blue, is it?" said Gale excitedly.

"We're in space all right—but it isn't glass you're looking through; it is fused quartz. Glass that thick would crack in a moment under the stress of temperature change it has to undergo. The sun looks blue because, for the first time in your life, you are seeing it without having more than half its light screened off. The atmosphere won't pass blue light completely and it cuts off the ultra-violet transmission very shortly after we leave the visible region of the spectrum. The reason the sun has always looked yellow is that you could never see that blue portion of its spectrum. Remember, a thing gets bluer and bluer as it gets hotter. First we have red hot, bright red, yellow, white, then the electric arc is so hot that it gives blue light. But the sun is nearly two thousand degrees centigrade hotter than the electric arc. Naturally it is blue. Also, I'll bet you haven't found Mars, have you?"

"No, Steve, I haven't. Where is it?"

"Right over there. See it?"

"But that can't be Mars. It's green, green as the Earth."

"But it is Mars. The reason Mars looks red from Earth is that the light that reaches us from Mars has had to go through both its own atmosphere and through ours, and by the time it reaches us, it is reddened, just as a distant plane beacon is. You know how a light in the distance looks red. That is what makes Mars look red."

"Mars is green. Then it is possible that the life on Mars may be the same as that of Earth!"

"Right, Dave. It probably is. Remember that the chlorophyll that gives the planets their color is also the material that can convert sunlight energy into fixed energy of starches and sugars for the plant, and probably the same material is serving in that capacity all over the universe, for carbon is the only element of the more than a hundred that there are that can possibly permit life's infinitely complicated processes to progress."

"But I thought there were only ninety-two elements."

"THERE are ninety-two different types of atoms, but if you have half a dozen men all doing exactly the same thing, can you call them 'a man'? They have found more than six different kinds of lead, two different kinds of chlorine, several different kinds of argon, and many of the other elements are really averages of several kinds of atoms, all of which do exactly the same thing, but have different weights, they are called isotopes. We say the atomic weight of chlorine is 35.457, but really there is no atom that has that weight. They have weights of 35 and 37, and are jumbled together so that the average is 35.457. Really there are over a hundred different kinds of atoms. In my work on this ship I found it made quite a difference which kind of chlorine atom I had."

"Well, how does this machine work, and what do you mean by saying that a machine invented it?"

"Dave, you know that for a number of years the greatest advances in physics have been made along the lines of mathematical work in atomic structure. Einstein was the greatest of the mathematicians, and so the greatest of the atomicists. Now as you well know, I never was too good at mathematics but I did love atomic structure, and I had some ideas, but I needed someone to work out the mathematics of the theory for me.

"You remember that back in 1929 in the Massachusetts Institute of Technology they had a machine they called the Integraph, an electrical machine that could do calculus too complex for Einstein himself to work out, and problems it would take Einstein months to solve, the machine could solve in a few minutes. It could actually do mathematics beyond the scope of the human brain. The calculus is a wonderful tool with which man can dig out knowledge, but he has to keep making his shovel bigger and bigger to dig deeper and deeper into the field of science. Toward the end of this decade, things got so the tail was wagging the dog to a considerable extent, the shovel was bigger than the man—we couldn't handle the tool. When that happened in the world once before they made a still bigger shovel, and hitched it to an electric motor. All the Integraph did was to hitch the calculus to an electric motor—and then things began to happen.

"I developed that machine further in my laboratory, and carried it far beyond the original plans. I can do with it a type of mathematics that was never before possible, and that mathematics, on that machine, has done something no man ever did. It has found the secret of the atom, and released for us atomic energy. But that wasn't all, the machine kept working at those great long equations, reducing the number of variables, changing, differentiating, integrating, and then I saw where it was leading! I was scared when I saw what those equations meant. I was afraid that the machine had made an error. I was deathly afraid to test that last equation, the equation which the machine was absolutely unable to change. *It had been working with the equations of matter, and now it had reached the ultimate, definitive equation of all matter!* This final equation gave explicit instructions to the understanding; it told just how to *completely destroy matter!* It told how to release such terrific energy. I was afraid to try it. The equations of atomic energy I had tested and found good. I had succeeded in releasing the energy of atoms.

"But the energy of matter has actually been known for many years; simple arithmetic can calculate the energy in one mere gram of matter. One gram is the equivalent of about ten drops of water and that much matter contains 900,000,000,000,000,000,000 ergs of energy, all this in ten drops of water! Mass is just as truly a measure of energy as ergs, as foot-pounds or as kilowatt-hours. You might buy your electricity by the pound. If you had five hundred million dollars or so, you could buy a pound. You have heard of atomic energy, of how terrifically powerful it is. It is just about one million times as great as the energy of coal. But that titanic energy is as little compared to the energy of matter itself, as the strength of an ant is compared to my strength. Material energy is ten thousand million times as great as the energy of coal. Perhaps now you can see why I was afraid to tryout those equations. One gram of matter could explode as violently as seven thousand tons of dynamite!

"But the machine was right. I succeeded in releasing that awful energy. I happened to release it as a heat ray, and the apparatus had been pointed in the direction of an open window luckily. Beyond that was just sand. The window was volatilized instantly, and the sand was melted to a great mass of fused quartz. It is there, and will be there for centuries, a two-mile streak of melted sand fifty feet broad! It makes a wonderful road of six-foot thick glass! The machine showed me a thousand ways to apply it. I am driving this ship by means of an interesting bit of apparatus that the calculating machine designed. You remember Einstein's general relativity theory said that mass, gravity, bent space; but as it didn't fall in, as it would if attracted and not resisting, it must be that it is elastic. The field theory that he brought out back in 1929 showed that gravity and electrostatic fields were at least similar. I found, with the aid of my machine, that they were very closely related. I charge the walls of my ship strongly negative, then I have a piece of apparatus here that will distort that electro-static field so it cuts off gravity—and the ship has no weight. The propulsion is simple also. I told you that space was elastic. I have a projector, or series of projectors all around the ship, which will throw a beam of a ray that tends to bend space toward it. The space resists, and since the mountain won't come to Mahomet, Mahomet goes to the mountain—and the ship sails along nicely.

"The only theoretical limit to my speed is, of course, the velocity of light. At that speed anybody would have infinite mass, and as you can't produce an infinite force, you certainly can't go any faster, and you can't go that fast in fact. If I accelerated one of the little five gram bullets I use in that machine gun to the speed of an alpha particle such as radium shoots off, not a very high speed in space, it would require as much energy to get it up to that speed, 10,000 miles a second, as five thousand fast freights, each a thousand tons apiece, would require to get up a speed of a mile a minute. You see that there is no possibility of getting up any speed like that even with material energy—it is too expensive even with that cheap energy—for it costs just as much to slow down again!

"The interesting thing about this energy is that scientists have known about it for a good many years, and while hundreds of people told about atomic energy, no one outside of the scientists ever spoke of the far greater energy of matter. The scientists said that the sun used that energy to maintain its heat—forty million degrees on the interior of the sun. They said man could never duplicate that temperature nor that pressure that prevails at the interior of the sun. They therefore said that man would never be able to release that energy. But the sun had to raise thousands of tons of water, and blow that vapor many miles, and do a lot of other complicated things before there was any lightning. Man would never be able to reproduce those conditions, and he would never be able to make lightning. Besides, if he did, what good would his electricity do him; it would be so wild, and so useless.

"But man discovered other ways of releasing his energies and converting it into electricity in a way that did not exist in nature. Manifestly it is possible to do the same with the energy of matter, and I have done it.

"The object of this trip, Dave, is exploration. I am going to the other planets, and I want you to come along. I believe I am prepared for any trouble we may meet there. That machine gun shoots bullets loaded with a bit of matter that will explode on impact. There is only a dust grain of it there, but it is as violent as ten tons of dynamite. If I exploded the entire shell, remember I would get the equivalent of thirty-five thousand tons of dynamite—which is manifestly unsafe. There are also a series of projectors around the car that project heat rays. These rays are capable of volatilizing anything that will absorb them. The projectors of all the rays have a separate generator unit directly connected. The unit is built right into the projector, but controlled from here. They are small, but tremendously more powerful than any power plant the Earth has ever seen before—each one can far outdo the great million-and-a-half horsepower station in San Francisco. They can develop in the neighborhood of fifty million horsepower each!"

"Lord, Steve, I'm no scientist, and when you speak glibly of power sources millions, billions of times more powerful than coal, I'm not only lost, I'm scared. And you have a couple dozen of those fifty-million-horsepower-generators around this ship. What would happen if they got short-circuited or something?"

"If they did, which I don't believe they will, they would either explode the entire ship, and incidentally make the Earth at least stagger in its orbit, or fuse it instantaneously and so destroy themselves. I might add that we would not survive the calamity."

"No. I rather guessed that. But, Steve, here in the utter cold and utter vacuum of space I should think that it would be hard to heat the ship. How do you do it?"

"The first thing to do in any explanation is to point out that space is neither empty nor cold. In the second place, a vacuum couldn't be either hot or cold. Temperature is a condition of matter, and if there is no matter, there can be no temperature. But space is quite full—about one atom per cubic inch. There is so much matter between us and the fixed stars that we can actually detect the spectrum of space superposed on the spectrum of the star. The light that the stars send us across the intervening spaces comes to us laden with a message of the contents of space—and tells of millions of tons of calcium and sodium. Even the tiny volume of our solar system contains in its free space about 125,000,000,000 grams of matter. That doesn't mean much to an astronomer—but when you remember that every gram of that can furnish as much energy as 10,000,000,000 grams of coal, we see that it isn't so little! And as space does have matter, it can have a temperature, and does. It has a temperature of about 15,000 degrees.

Most of the atoms of that space have escaped from the surface of stars and have a temperature about the same as that of the surface of the stars. So you see that space—utterly cold—is hotter than anything on Earth! The only difficulty is that it takes a whale of a lot of space to contain enough atoms to weigh a gram, and so the average concentration of heat is so low that we can say that space is cold. Similarly a block of ice may contain far more heat than a piece of red-hot iron. Nevertheless, I would prefer to sit on the ice."

"Quite so. I see your point, and I believe I'd prefer the ice myself. But that's interesting! Space isn't empty; it's not cold—in fact it is unusually hot!"

"Now we've started this let's finish it, Dave. It is hot, but not unusually hot—if anything it is unusually cold! The usual, or average temperature of all the matter in the universe is about one million degrees, so space at 15,000 is really far below the average, and so we can say that it is unusually cold. The temperature of the interior of the stars is uniformly forty million degrees, which brings the average up. But it is the unthinkably great quantities of matter in interstellar space that brings the average down. Remember that the nearest star is four and a half light years from us, and between the stars there is such a vast space in which the matter is thinly distributed that the few pinpoint concentrations of matter have to be extremely hot if they are to bring the average up any appreciable amount. But here and there in this vast space there are a few tiny bits of matter that have cooled down to terrifically frigid temperatures—temperatures within a few degrees of absolute zero, only two or three hundred degrees above; spots of matter so cold that hydrogen and oxygen can unite; so cold that this compound can even condense to a liquid; so cold that life can exist. We call those pinpoints planets.

"In the interstellar range of temperatures we have everywhere from absolute zero to forty million above. Life can exist between the temperatures absolute, of about two hundred and three hundred and twenty—a range of one hundred degrees in a range of forty million. That means that the temperature of this planet must be maintained with an allowable inaccuracy of one part in four hundred thousand! Do you see what the chances of a planet's having a 'habitable' temperature are?

"But we are near my laboratory now, Dave, and I want to introduce you to Wright, my laboratory assistant, a brilliant student, and an uncannily clever artisan. He made Bartholemew, as I call the mathematics machine, and most of the parts of this ship. He had heat rays to work with, and had iridium metal as his material, and plenty of any element. He had a fine time working out the best alloy, and the best treatment. The shell of the car is made of an alloy of tungsten, iridium, and cobalt. It is exceedingly tough, very strong, and very hard. It will scratch glass, is stronger than steel, and is as ductile and malleable as copper—if you have sufficient force. Iridium used to sell for about 250 dollars an ounce, but these powers allow me to transmute it, which renders it cheap for me. After this, sodium metal will be cheaper than sodium compounds!"

"I wish that that trip had not been so short, Steve. There were a lot of things I wanted to ask you. Where are we now? I don't seem to recognize this country."

"We are over Arizona—see there is the laboratory now—off there."

"What? Arizona! How fast were we going?"

"We were going slowly, considering we were in space, but considering our proximity to the Earth we are going rapidly. The actual speed is difficult to determine—remember we had cut loose all ties of gravity, and I had to follow the Earth in its orbit, and the whole solar system along through space. From here to New York City is about three thousand miles, and as we made the trip in just under one hundred minutes, we traveled at a speed of thirty miles a minute, or half a mile a second."

"Well, the airplane speed record was about four hundred and twenty, wasn't it—I mean an hour—you have to specify now! You set a new record, I guess!"

# CHAPTER TWO

THEY were slanting down through the atmosphere toward the distant low building that had seen the construction of that first of Earth's space cruisers. The long gentle glide slowly flattened out and the car at last glided slowly, gently through the open hangar doors. Wright was there to greet them, but Waterson called out that he would stay in the ship a few minutes to show Gale around.

"Steve, you sure picked a desolate place to work in. Why did you go way out here?"

"For two reasons. First I wanted a place that was quiet; and second I wanted a place where I could safely work with atomic energy—where explosions, premeditated or accidental, would not blow up an entire city. Did you notice that crater off to one side as we came in? That is where I tried out my first bullet. I hadn't gotten a small enough charge in it. I had nearly a milligram—a hundredth of a drop of water. But come, I guess you saw the pilot room. I'll show you how to run the ship tomorrow."

He led the way to the rear end of the pilot room, where a small door opened in the smooth, windowless metal partition. It too gleamed with that strangely iridescent beauty of metallic iridium.

"This bunk room should appeal to an apartment house addict. I had about eleven feet I could use to make it, and it is just a bit crowded."

Considering Waterson's six-feet-two, a room eleven feet long, ten feet high, and about as wide, would certainly be crowded if there was anything or anyone else in the room. As the bunkroom was also dining room, gallery, and chart room, it was decidedly crowded. One thing that particularly interested Gale was a small screen on which were a series of small lights, projected from the rear.

"What is that, Steve?" he inquired.

"That is my chart. It is the only kind of a chart you could well expect on board a spaceship. The lights are really moving and maintain the relative positions of the planets. I think we will go to Mars first, because it is now as close as it will be for some time. I want to go to Venus soon, but that is on the other side of the sun. I will find that there are detours even in space when I go there!"

"That's quite a chart! I suppose you have more accurate ones too?"

"No. I have no need of more accurate ones. I start for my objective, and it's so big I can't miss it!"

"That's true, too! But I haven't seen any apparatus for taking care of your air. I suspect that door over there hides something."

"It does. It leads to the storeroom and the apparatus room. There are all the tools I carry, the air purifier and water renewer. Remember that the break-up of the atomic energy gives me unlimited amounts of electricity, so I have all the electric power I can use. I find that there is a way to electrolyze carbon dioxide to carbon and oxygen. In this manner I recover the oxygen for the air—at least part of the necessary oxygen—and at the same time remove the menace of the $CO_2$. There is considerable oxygen fixed as $H_2O$, however, so I installed an electrolyzer to take care of that. The moisture of the air is in this way kept down to a comfortable maximum. The same apparatus is useful for reducing the water. All the water I have I must carry in tanks, which require space. I am able to make them considerably smaller by taking the water, passing it through this electrolyzer, reducing it to hydrogen and oxygen, burning them to water again, and thus getting pure $H_2O$.

"The one difficulty is in getting rid of the heat. Remember that all the heat I lose I must lose by radiation. But the sun is radiating to me. I receive heat at exactly the same rate the Earth does and I have no protective atmosphere, so the tendency is to reach a super-tropical temperature. The easiest solution of this problem is to go with the ship at such an angle to the sun that the shadow of the exposed surface shades the greater portion of the ship, then by adjusting the angle of the ship. I can adjust the ratio of radiating to receiving area to any value I wish, and get almost any temperature I need."

"That is an idea. I never heard of electrolyzing carbon dioxide, though. Tell me—how do you do it?"

"That is a process I developed. It requires considerable explaining. However, I am doubtful whether it wouldn't have been easier to convert the stuff directly to oxygen by transmutation."

"Steve, I notice you have plenty of light, but why not have windows?"

"I HAVE no windows except in the main pilot room. The trouble with windows is that they reduce the strength of the shell. Also, as this is a sleeping room, and there will be no night in space, why not have it this way? I need considerable strength in the walls of the ship, because the accelerations that I use in starting and turning and stopping are really rather a strain on any material. The outer wall is a six-inch iridio-tungsten alloy shell, with two openings in it, the window, and the door. The rest is absolutely seamless, one solid casting. The window is so designed, in connection with the placement of the ray projectors, that it doesn't weaken the shell. There is no framework, but the two partitions across the ship are each six inches thick, and act as braces. The inner wall is a thin one-inch layer of metal, supported by the outer shell, and separated from it by small braces about two inches high. This intervening space has been evacuated by the simple process of going out into space and opening a valve, then closing it before returning to Earth."

"That one-inch layer of metal of yours is bothering me. There is something strange about it, and all the trim and moldings in here. The green I suppose is to relieve eyestrain, but it is not the color itself that seems strange. It is the impression I have that the metal itself is of that beautiful leaf green shade, and that it is the metal in the chairs, table, and racks that gives them that color."

"Quite right Dave, it is."

"But Steve, I thought that there were no more elements to be discovered. In the collection at the Museum in New York they had all ninety-two, and I saw no colored metals."

"In the first place, remember I told you there really were more than ninety-two elements, if we treat the isotopes as elements, and I don't believe they had all the ninety-two there, for there are several elements that disintegrate inside of a few days. They couldn't keep those. But these metals are compounds."

"Compounds! Do you mean alloys?"

"No, chemical compounds, just as truly as salt or sulfuric acid. They are related to tetra ethyl stibine, $Sb(C_2H_5)_4$, which is a compound that acts like a metal, physically and chemically. It is too soft to be any good, but there are hundreds of these organic compounds of carbon. There are red ones, green ones, blue ones, and a thousand different ones, soft, brittle, liquid, solid; some are even gaseous."

"Colored metals! What a boon to artists! Think what fun they will have working in that stuff!"

"Yes, but it is also useful for decorative purposes, although the large molecule makes it too soft to be used as a wearing surface."

"Well Steve, you sure have a mighty fine little ship! What do you call it? You said that you called the mathematics machine 'Bartholemew.' What do you call this?"

"As yet it has not been named. I wanted you to suggest some name for it."

"That's a sudden order, Steve. What have you thought of?"

"Well, I thought of calling it *Flourine*, for the chemical element which is so active that it cannot be displaced by any other, but will, on the other hand, force any other non-metal out of its compound. Then I thought of *Nina*, the name of Columbus' ship which first touched a new world, and Wright reminded me that Eric the Red's son, Lief, landed here in about 1000 and suggested Eric as a name."

"Well, that's a good assortment. Why pick on me?"

"We thought you ought to be good at inventing names, since you had written several books."

"That's a fine excuse! I get mine from old magazines! But I might suggest *The Electron*. It sounds well, and I remember that you said that you charged it negatively to cut out the gravity of the Earth and an electron—or is it a proton that has a negative charge?"

"*The Electron*—sounds good—and the idea is good. An electron has a negative charge. Wright also suggested the *Terrestrian*, as it would be the first ship of Earth to visit other worlds. It is between *Electron* and *Terrestrian* now. Which do you like better?"

"I prefer *Terrestrian*. It has more meaning."

"Well, we'll tell Wright about it. In the mean time, come in to the laboratory and meet Bartholemew."

BARTHOLEMEW was at the moment engaged in tracing a very complicated curve, the integral of a half dozen or so other curves. Wright was carefully watching the thin line left by the pencil. There was a low steady humming coming from the machine, and a bank of small transformers on the other side of the room connected to it. Wright turned off the machine as they entered, and after greeting Waterson, and meeting Gale, proceeded at once with an enthusiastic description of the machine. He was obviously proud of the machine, and of the man who had developed it. The entire machine had been enclosed in a metal case when Gale entered, but now Wright opened this, and Gale was decidedly surprised to see the interior. He really had had no reason to form any opinion of the machine, but he had expected a maze of gears, shafts, levers, chains, and every sort of mechanical apparatus. Somehow the mention of a machine for doing mathematics conveyed to him that impression. The actual machine seemed quite simple merely a small cable leading from the separate "graph interpreters," as Wright called them, to the central integrator, and hence a small motor carried the integrated result into practice and put it on paper.

This machine made possible a type of mathematics hitherto unknown. This new calculus was to the previous integration what integration was to addition. Integration is an infinite summation of very small terms, and this new mathematics was an integration in an infinite number of dimensions. The beginner first learns to integrate in two dimensions. Then come three. Einstein had carried his mathematics to four. The machine seemed to work in an infinite number of dimensions, but the conditions of the problem really chose the four out of infinity that were under discussion. An infinite number of dimensions has no physical meaning. It might be put this way, Wright said:

there are an infinite number of solutions to the equation x=2+y, and as such it has no meaning. But if for example you say also that 2y=x, then auto-mathematically you choose two of an infinite number of values that fit the problem in hand. A man might have done all this machine did, had he lived long enough and been patient enough. This machine could do in an hour a problem that would have taken a man a lifetime. Thus it had been able to develop the true mathematical picture of the atom.

# CHAPTER THREE

OVER the supper table that night they had a final discussion as to the name of the ship. It was decided that the name should be *Terrestrian,* and plans were made to christen it in as scientific a manner as possible. Considering that the shell was made of iridium, and therefore highly inert to chemical action, they decided on a bottle of aqua regia, which dissolves gold and platinum, and does not attack iridium. A bottle was prepared, and they were ready for the christening in the morning. Just as they decided to call the day done, the telephone rang. It was Dr. Wilkins of Mt. Wilson calling Waterson. The conversation was rather lengthy, and Wright, who had answered, told Gale that Dr. Wilkins had called before, about two months ago, on a question in astro-physics, and Waterson had been able to give the answer. This time however, Dr. Wilkins, it seemed, was greatly agitated. Just then Waterson returned.

"Gale, it seems we chose our name well. Also I am lucky in having you here. I must go to Mt. Wilson at once. I'll be back about dawn, and I'll tell you two all about it then. I've got to hurry. So long."

A moment later the two men heard the hum of the motor as the hangar doors were opened. Another moment and the entire countryside was flooded with a blaze of bluish white light that illuminated the desolate dry desert for miles, and for all those weary miles it was an unending, rolling surface of sand. In the glow of sudden light, great strange shadows, which started up by the buildings, gave weird effects on the sand, but with it all there was a rugged and compelling beauty to the little world that the light had cut from the darkness.

There was a sudden whistle of air, and the light faded as the car shot off toward Mt. Wilson.

"What a mass of sand there is around here! It would seem almost like a dried up ocean bed," said Gale.

"I suppose there is a lot of sand in the world—there should be though, it is the direct compound of the two most abundant elements on Earth, silicon and oxygen."

"Wright. I've often wondered why it is that oxygen, which combines with almost anything, should be found free in nature. Why is it?"

"I'm sure I don't know. At that I suppose one reason is that there is so much of it. It forms over forty-nine per cent of it to a depth of ten miles at least. It is the second most active element on Earth—in the universe for that matter, and of the active elements there is only one with which it can't combine, namely, fluorin. Of course it can't combine with the inert gases, so I say the active elements. I suppose it is left free principally because there was nothing else to do. Apparently there weren't enough partners to go around. At that it did a mighty good job of it! Forty-seven per cent of the solid crust is oxygen, 85% of the water is oxygen, and 20% of the air is free oxygen. Well, let's not look so favorable a gift horse in the mouth. If it hadn't been left free, where would we be?"

The discussion soon died down and the men retired for the night, each wondering what it was that had called Waterson away so suddenly, and each determined to be on hand when he returned in the morning.

The coming of the light of dawn had, perforce, put an end to the activities at Mt. Wilson, so it was shortly after sunrise that the two men heard the hangar doors open. And it was very shortly after sunrise that they had dressed and gone down to greet Waterson. The worried look on his face told a great deal, for both men knew him well, and when Waterson looked worried there was something of tremendous import under way.

"Hello. Had a good night, Dave? I have something that is going to interest you—and two and a half billion other human beings. They have discovered something at the Mt. Wilson observatory that is going to change our plans quite a bit. We had intended going to other planets to visit the inhabitants, but we won't have to go. They are coming to us; furthermore, twenty ships are coming, and I have an idea they are good-sized ships. But Wright, I think you had better start breakfast. We can discuss it at the table. I'm going to wash, and if you will help Wright, Dave, I think we will be at work pretty soon." Waterson left the room, and the two men looked at his retreating figure with astonishment and wonder. An announcement that our planet was to be invaded from outer space is a bit hard to take in all at once, and particularly when it is given in the matter of fact way that Waterson had presented it, for he had known it now for over ten hours, and had been working on it during all that time.

At the table the explanation was resumed. "The ships were first sighted in the big telescope when they turned it toward Mars last night. You remember that Mars is at its closest now, and they are taking a good many pictures of it. When they saw these spots of light on the disc of Mars they were at once excited and started immediate spectroscopic and radiometric observations. The fact that they showed against the disc of Mars meant that they were nearer than the planet, and by measuring the amount of energy coming from them they tried to calculate their size. The results at once proved that they could not be light because of reflection, for the energy that they emitted would require a surface of visible dimensions, and these were points. Their temperature was too low to be incandescent, so they were violating all the laws of astro-physics. By this time they had shifted sufficiently to make some estimate of their distance, shifted because of the movement of the Earth in its orbit, Dave, and so they were covering a different spot on the disc of Mars. Allowing that they were going in a straight line, they were some ten and a half million miles away. The spectroscope showed by displacement of one of the spectral lines that they were coming toward us at about 100 miles a second. The line of their flight was such that they would intercept the Earth in its orbit in about thirty hours. That means that we have about twenty to work in.

"It doesn't take any alarmist to guess that this means trouble. They would not be coming in twenty ships if they were coming on a peaceful mission. Also considering that they come in only twenty ships it shows that they have considerable confidence in those twenty. Since they are coming here without first sending a scouting party of one or two ships, I suspect that they already know that the conditions of Earth are suitable to them. To determine our conditions would require exceedingly powerful telescopes, but they are helped by the thin air of their planet. I believe that they can actually see our machines and weapons, and that they know just about what we have. I think that they are counting on cleaning up the world very easily—as indeed they would but for one factor, for they have atomic energy. Wright, do you remember that we decided to use electronic rockets to drive the car, once we discovered atomic energy? And that having discovered material energy, we naturally decided not to? Well, they have electronic rockets. This makes me feel sure that that means that they have atomic energy, but have no material energy."

"Fine Steve. Your reasoning is most admirable—but will you please translate 'electronic rocket' and a few of those other terms into English? And otherwise make yourself clear to the layman?"

"Well, I suppose I have no right to call a cathode ray tube an electronic rocket, but when a cathode ray tube gets that big it really needs a new name. The idea is the same as that of a rocket. You know the experiments the Germans, the millionaire Opel, and others carried out in 1927 with rocket automobiles? They had a terrible time with their rockets because the heat of one set off the next. The result was a disastrous explosion—and they had a whole ocean of air to cool them! What would a rocket do in free space?

"Also remember the principle of a rocket is that you shoot particles out of the rear at a very high speed and thus impart the kick to the ship. The electronic rocket does the same thing—but instead of shooting molecules of hot gas, it shoots electrons, a giant cathode ray tube such as Coolidge had in 1927, but his was so small that the kick was immeasurable. Remember that as the velocity of the electrons approaches that of light, the mass increases and so the electrons as shot from a cathode ray rocket may weigh as much as a milligram. The problem of propulsion then is not hard with atomic energy to supply the terrific voltages needed to run the tube. But the cathode rays are going to be their first weapon.

"Cathode rays are absorbed by any object they hit, and their terrific energy is converted to heat. They are deadly in themselves, and the heat is of course deadly. They will also have heat rays. I can make a heat ray with atomic energy, though mine is derived from material. The only way we can fight them is to know beforehand what we are to meet.

This is to be a war for a world, and the war will be a battle of titanic forces. The weaker of the forces will be a million times greater than anything man has ever known before, and either of these two forces would, if fully applied, blast our planet from its place around the sun! Such forces cannot be withstood. They must be annulled, deflected, or annihilated by some greater force. Only when we know what to expect can we fight them, and live. Remember, if they once succeeded in getting one weak spot in our armor, we can never have another chance, and the world can never hope to fight them—mere armies and a navy or two, with a couple of air forces thrown in—what would they amount to? The energy of atoms could destroy them like paper in a blow-torch—think what would happen to one of those beautifully absorbing grey battleships if a heat ray touched it! Their eighteen-inch steel armor would not melt—it would boil away! A submarine would be no safer—they could explode the water about it into steam and crush it. The effect of a heat ray in water is just that—the water is converted to steam so suddenly that there is a terrific explosion. The cathode rays could sweep an army out of existence as a hose might wash away an army of mud soldiers.

"They won't have gases. They will have no use for them. They could wipe a city off the map, leave only a great crater in the scarred Earth, while men were getting ready to lay a gas barrage. A shell would certainly just bounce off of the armor of my ship and I suspect that it would do the same with the Martian ships.

"Earth has only one weapon that can even bother them! And that one weapon is the one factor they did not figure on! It is the *Terrestrian.* But now, if we want to make that one factor upset the whole equation, we have to calculate how to make its value a maximum, and to do that we have to know every other factor in the equation. I have suggested two weapons they will have, the cathode rays and the heat ray. They will, of course, have others; they will have atomic bombs, and I am sure that they will find us so dangerous that they will be willing to lose a ship and crash us. This gives us something else to avoid. Can any of you think of something else?"

"Good Lord Steve, haven't you thought of enough?"

"Plenty, Dave, but it isn't considered good form in military proceedings to permit the enemy to surprise you. In fact, it is highly probable that if he does, you will get a new form, one more adapted to aerial transit."

"Yes, that's true, too. But I remember reading once that ultra-violet light was invisible, and very dangerous to the body. I wonder if they will use that?"

"They may, but I greatly doubt it. Air is very nearly opaque to ultra-violet light, above a certain limit, and below that limit it is not very harmful. The infrared heat rays, though, are going to be a very great menace. I can't think of any way to make them harmless. Of course, the polished iridium shell of the ship will protect us from the sides, as the heat will all be reflected. The difficulty will be that the heat will fuse the window, and thus attack us. The quartz glass is nearly opaque to heat rays, as is all glass. Being opaque, it absorbs it, 'cuts it out' as we say. The result will be that the glass will melt instantly, whereupon we will go very quickly. The idea of putting a polished metal shutter before the window is the one we will have to adopt, but we must modify it somehow. The heat rays will be turned back all right—and so will the light rays. The question is to shut out heat and let in light. Any suggestions?"

"I wonder if there isn't some selective reflector that we could use, Dr. Waterson?"

"That is a good idea, Wright—but I don't know of any that will pass all the light and reflect all the heat!"

"What is a selective reflector, Steve?"

"There are lots of things that have that property Dave; gold leaf is one, it can transmit green light—that is you can see green light through it, but it reflects yellow light—the complement of the green it transmits. There are a great many organic dyes that are one color when you look at them and the complement of that color when you look through them.

The trouble is we need one that transmits the visible portion of the spectrum and—boy—that's it, Wright, that's it—spectrum—take a totally reflecting diffraction grating, reflect out all that part of the spectrum that we don't want, take what we do, pass it through a prism to recombine it to white light, then through lenses so we can see as if through a telescope! We will have absolutely cold light!"

"Again it sounds good, but I'd like to hear it in English, Steve."

"The idea is to take a diffraction grating, a piece of metal with, usually, 14,438 lines to the inch ruled on it, and previously highly polished, so that it reflects most of the light that hits it. Now it is reflected at different angles, so that we have a spectrum. The spectrum spreads out light and heat waves as well—I use the reflection grating as no material will pass the heat rays, and it then is possible to reflect out of the car again those rays we do not want. The light, which we do want, we will pass through a prism, which will recombine it to white light. A prism can either split up light into different colors, or recombine them to white. Lenses then will be needed to make the images clear. The effect will be much the same as a telescope. And that takes care of the heat waves. The cathode rays, luckily won't bother us, for the car is already charged strongly negative, and negatively charged electrons will be strongly repelled, as they are in the grid of a vacuum tube, so will never hit us. The bombs constitute the worst menace. The only defense we have against them is the very doubtful one of not being there when they are. That is a good policy in any case.

"As a last precaution—a bit grim—I will arrange it so that if the *Terrestrian* is damaged to the point of utter helplessness we can, by pushing a single button, explode the entire car—as material energy. It will utterly destroy everything within a radius of a hundred miles, and damage everything within a much greater radius. I believe it will not be serious enough to change the Earth's orbit, though."

"Good—cheerful man, aren't you, Steve! Now what have we to meet that delightful array?"

"We have things even more delightful. Our heat ray is considerably more powerful, I imagine. It is generated by a force ten thousand times as great. Our bombs will be worse. Wright, I wish you would make about a hundred shells that will explode with the full thirty-five thousand ton equivalent of dynamite. And then we will have everything they have that is going to be effective, and have it in a more concentrated form. Can any of you suggest anything else?"

"Steve, you said that your car was nearly pure iridium on the outside, and that is very inert. The outside of their ship will be polished too, won't it?"

"Probably—though I don't believe they were expecting to meet a heat ray."

"Well, I wonder if there isn't some chemical you could spray out that would tarnish their ship, without hurting your iridium ship? Then it wouldn't be polished and would absorb your heat rays."

"That's a good idea, Dave. I might use a sulfide—nearly all sulfides are colored, and form very easily and rapidly. Or I might use liquid ozone. That will tarnish almost anything to an oxide, which is also apt to be colored. I could certainly heat the ship that way, but I wonder—I'm afraid that the oxide or sulfide would break down too easily. There is only one metal that they might use on which that would work, namely steel. Iron sulfide is black, stable, and will not decompose readily. The oxide forms readily, is highly colored, and will not decompose before the metal is incandescent, or even melted. The only difficulty is that steel is so readily attacked, that they wouldn't use it. They would probably coat it with an inert metal, silver for instance.

That forms a black sulfide very readily. I'm afraid that won't work Dave. But Wright, I think that it would be a good idea to develop a few of those field theory equations in a different way. Try integrating number two-six-thirty-nine— I think that's it—and between the limits of equation one-four-twenty-three and zero. I have an idea that a little development of that idea will give us a beam that will be very useful. We haven't time to make much apparatus, but I think the result will be near enough to the space-curving projector to allow us to change the extra projectors we have in the laboratory to fit. Also, try calculating the arrangement we will need for the heat eliminator, please. I'm going to give Dave his first lesson in space navigation. We'll be back about noon—if at all!" But Gale caught the wink, so the effect was lost.

# CHAPTER FOUR

TEN thousand miles out in free space the practice began. As Waterson pointed out, it would require some mighty poor handling to hit the Earth now. For the first time in Gale's life he could practice with a machine with no fear of hitting anything.

When the ship slanted down in a long graceful glide, to enter the hangar doors that noon, Gale was in control. The controls of the ship were remarkably easy to master and extremely simple. The one thing that was hard to master was the tremendous range of power. It could be changed in a smooth climb from a fraction of a horsepower to billions! The first attempts had been a bit hard on the passengers, the seat straps coming in for their share of use.

When they returned to the laboratory, they found Wright had just prepared a light lunch, and at once began to demolish it. Six hours between breakfast and lunch is conducive to a husky appetite.

Wright had finished the integration on the machine, and had calculated the mathematics of the heat eliminator in a little less than four hours. The results were very satisfactory, and in the remaining time he had converted six of the extra projectors to their new use, and had them ready for installation. After lunch the men began on the construction of the heat eliminators. Two were to be installed, one for the observer as well as one for the pilot. The heavier work of installing the projectors and the iridium shield was reserved for later in the afternoon.

By six that evening, the new projectors were completely installed and the connections made, and the great iridium shield was cooling from blinding incandescence in its mold. It would be installed that night, but now they felt that a rest and a meal were due them. They had been working under a great strain that afternoon, for they knew that they must get that machine ready before the Martians reached Earth, and there was a great deal to do. After the brief dinner they went out to the shining *Terrestrian*. As yet, the new projectors had not been tried.

Gracefully the great shining shell backed out into the ruddy glory of the sinking sun, the red light had turned the desert to a sea of rolling fire, with here and there a wave that showed dark—a mound. In the far distance the purple hills of Nevada seemed like distant islands in this burning sea, and above it rode this lone, shining ship, magnificently iridescent in the setting-sun. Now it stopped, hovered, then suddenly a pile of metal ingots that lay to one side of the laboratory leaped into the air and shot toward it—then paused in mid-air, hung poised for an instant, then sank lightly to the ground. Now the sand of the desert began to roll into some strange wave that began just beneath the ship, then sped away—further—till it died in the far distance, by means of an invisible beam. A wall of sand thirty feet high had been built in an instant, and it extended as far as the eye could reach! Now the ship settled, and slowly, light as a feather for all its three thousand tons of metal, it glided into the hangar.

"Man Steve, that works! How long a range has it? And please tell me about it now you are sure it works!"

"I don't know just how long a range it has—it affected the sand as far as we could see, and we were using very little power. It is just a modification of the space curving apparatus. It projects a beam of gravity, and theoretically at least it has an infinite range; and it certainly has a whale of a lot of power. I can use a good deal of the power too, for the strain of the attraction is taken off the mountings and the ship, and put on space itself! The gravity projector is double and projects a beam of the gravity ray forward and an equally powerful beam of the space curve behind. The two rays are controlled by the same apparatus, and so are always equal. The result is that no matter how great a load I put on it, the entire load is expended in trying to bend space!"

Illustrations by
H. W. Wesso

That night work was carried on under the floodlighting from the ship's great light projectors. The entire region was illuminated, and work was easy. Waterson had been instructed to take a rest when he seemed bent on continuing his work. Even his great body could not keep up that hard labor forever, and forty-eight hours of work will make any man nervous. With a crisis such as this facing him, he certainly needed rest. He agreed, provided they would call him in two hours.

Two hours later Gale walked about a mile from the laboratory and called. He then returned and continued his work on the placement of the shield. It had been placed, polished, and tiny holes bored in it for the heat eliminator inside of four hours. It was operated by an electric motor, controlled from within. It could be lowered and leave the window clear, but when in position its polished surface made it perfectly safe against heat rays. The work had just been completed, when Waterson reappeared looking decidedly ruffled.

"Say, I thought you two promised to call me in two hours! It's been just four, and I woke up myself!"

"But Steve, I did call you and you didn't hear me. I didn't say I'd wake you in two hours."

IT was shortly afterwards that news of the coming invasion was made public. And with the news came the wild panics, even mad, licentious outbreaks all over the world. Man saw himself helpless before mighty enemies whom he could not resist. Never had such a complete disruption of business taken place in so short a time. Things were done that night in a terrible spirit of "we die tomorrow, we play today." The terrible jams in the cities caused the deaths of hundreds of thousands. They wanted to flee the cities, get into the woods and hide like some animal. Within an hour no news could reach most of them, and though Waterson had told of his ship, told immediately, given every government official announcements concerning it, still the mad dance went on. But to those that had stayed near the radio sets, this news brought relief. No television pictures of it could be broadcast for many hours, as there was no portable equipment within several hundreds of miles, and the men were working on the ship.

That night the three men took turns watching by the radio set for news. The Martians were due to land somewhere on Earth that morning. It would probably be a temporary landing in some land that was just at dawn. And it was so. But the *Terrestrian* must not be taken by surprise.

Waterson was to have the morning watch. Unlike the others, he did not sit by the radio set. He answered the few messages he received, but the entire four hours of his watch he spent working with Bartholemew. "The equations he was working with seemed new, strange, and they had terrific import to the understanding. It was but a few minutes before the Martians landed when he had gotten the final result. At once he called the two others.

"Wright, if that equation means what I think it does, we have something that will give us a tremendous advantage! I feel sure that the Martians have actually worked out the problem of the atom by pure brainpower—no machines aided them, else they too would have discovered the secret of matter. That machine has made it possible for us to work out problems to meet them. But as they may land any minute now, let's begin on this: We need two of these projectors in front, and two at the stern. If you will start on the actual projectors, I'll start the instrument end. Come on Dave."

And so all three heard the announcement that the Martians had landed. Twenty mighty ships had settled down in the arid land of Nevada. The ships were a bare five hundred miles from them! The dry air of the desert was probably best suited for Martian lungs. Army planes had been cruising about all night waiting for the enemy, waiting to learn definitely what they were to face. It was Lt. Charles H. Austin who sighted them. He first saw them while still on the very outskirts of our atmosphere, and reported them at once, turning his television finder on them.

Great balls of purple fire they seemed as they sank rapidly through our atmosphere. The great ships floated down and as they came within a mile or so of him, he was able to see that the great flaming globes of light were beneath them, seemingly supporting them. A breeze was blowing from them to him, and the air, even at that distance, was chokingly impregnated with oxides of nitrogen and ozone, from the forty mighty glowing spheres. They were fully an hundred and fifty feet in diameter, but the ships themselves, illuminated by the weird light of the glow of their sister ships, were far greater.

Each was three thousand feet long, and two hundred and fifty feet in diameter. Hundreds of thousands of tons those mighty machines must have weighed, and the fiery globes of ionized air that shone under the impact of the cathode rays alone told how they were supported. Now, two by two they sank, and came to rest on the sands below, and as they came near the ground the glowing ray touched the sand, and for that moment it glowed incandescent, then quickly cooled as the ray was shut off.

At last the mighty armada of space had settled on the packed sands, and now there sprang from each a great shaft of light that searched the heavens above for planes. By luck the plane of the observer was missed, and the television set clicked steadily on as the questing beams were reduced to five, and now the ground was flooded with blinding light. A moment later the side of one of the great ships opened, and from it a gangplank thrust itself. Then from it there came a stream of men, but men with great chests, great ears, thin arms and legs; men that must have stood ten feet high. Painfully they scrambled down the plank, toiling under the greater gravity of Earth. But what a thrill must have been theirs! They were the first men of this system to ever have set foot on two planets! And some of those men were to step forth on a third—the first men to visit it too!

Painfully now they were coming from their huge interplanetary cruisers, slowly they plodded across the intervening space to their comrades pouring from their sister ships.

THEN suddenly the television screen was white—a blinding searchlight had at last picked up the plane. Wildly the pilot dived, and now there came a picture of all those men looking upward, their first glimpse of the works of man perhaps. But the beam that had been eluded was reinforced in a moment—then there came a dull red beam—a flash—and the screen was smoothly dark.

Waterson and his friends feverishly worked at their tasks. There was no doubt about the inimical intentions of the Martians now. They had destroyed a man without reason. And the projectors were rapidly taking shape under the practiced hands of Wright. Dawn broke, and the men stopped for breakfast, but still the work on the projectors was not done. Many parts were so similar to those of the other projectors that they could use the spare projectors for parts, many others were new.

It was shortly after breakfast that the news of the Martians' landing came. They had started now on the famous Day of Terror. But still the men in the laboratory worked at their tasks. The *Terrestrian* had been christened according to plan, and was now ready to start at any moment, but the new projectors were an additional weapon—a mighty weapon.

All matter is made of atoms, grouped to form molecules, combinations of atoms, or a molecule may contain but one atom, as is the case of helium. The atoms within the molecule are held to each other by electro-static attraction. The molecules of substances like wood are very large, and hold to each other by a form of gravity between the molecules. These are called amorphous substances. Water is a liquid, a typical liquid, but we have many things that we do not recognize as liquids. Asphalt may be so cold that it will scarcely run, yet we can say it is a liquid. Glass is a liquid. It is a liquid that has cooled till it became so viscous it could not run. Glass is not crystalline, but after very many years it does slowly crystallize. The molecules of a liquid are held together by a gravitational attraction for each other. But in crystals we have a curious condition. The atoms of salt, sodium chloride, do not pair off one sodium and one chlorine atom when they crystallize; perhaps a million sodium atoms go with a million chlorine atoms, and give a crystal of sodium chloride. Thus we have that a crystal is not $n(NaC1)$ but it is $Na_nCl_n$. Thus a crystal of salt is one giant molecule. This means then that the crystal is held together by electrostatic forces and not gravitational forces. The magnitude of these forces is such that if equivalent weights of sodium and chlorine atoms could be separated and placed at the poles, the chlorine atoms at the north and, eight thousand miles to the south, the sodium, over all that distance the twenty-three pounds of sodium would attract the thirty-five pounds of chlorine atoms with a force of forty tons!

So it is that in all crystals the atoms are mutually balancing, and balanced by perhaps a dozen others. The electrostatic forces hold the crystals together, and the crystals then hold together by gravity in many cases; otherwise they don't hold together at all. A block of steel is made of billions of tiny crystals, each attracting its neighbor, and thus are held together. But this force is a gravitational force.

Now what would happen if the force of gravity between these crystals were annihilated? Instantly the piece of metal would cease to have any strength; it would fall to a heap of ultra-microscopic crystals, a mere heap of impalpably fine dust! The strongest metal would break down to nothing!

Such was the ray that Waterson had developed! It would throw a beam of a force that would thus annul the force of gravity, and the projector had been made of a single crystal of quartz. Its effects could be predicted, and it would indeed be a deadly weapon! The hardest metals fell to a fine powder before it. Wood, flesh, liquids, any amorphous or liquid substance was thrown off as single molecules. It would cause water to burst into vapor spontaneously, without heat, for when there is no attraction between the molecules, water is naturally a gas. Only crystals defied this disintegration ray, and only crystals could be used in working with it.

But while the men in the lonely laboratory in Arizona were finishing the most terrible of their weapons, the Martians were going down the Pacific coast.

When morning dawned on our world, it found a wild and restless aggregation of men fleeing wildly from every large city, and with dawn came the news that the Martian armada had risen, taking all its ships, and was heading westward. Straight across Nevada they sailed in awful grandeur, the mighty globes of blazing cathode rays bright even in the light of the sun.

Across the eastern part of California, and with an accuracy that told of carefully drawn maps, they went directly to the largest city of the West Coast, San Francisco. There they hung, high in air, their mighty glowing spheres a magnificent sight, motionless, like some mighty menace that hangs, ever ready to fall in terrible doom on the victim beneath. For perhaps an hour they hung thus, motionless, then there dropped from them the first of the atomic bombs. Tiny they were. No man saw them fall; only the effects were visible, and they were visible as a mighty chasm yawned in sudden eruption where solid earth had been before. One landed in the Golden Gate. After that it looked as a child's dam might look—a wall of mud and pebbles. But pictures and newsreels of the destruction of that city tell far more than any wordy description can. Once it had been destroyed by earthquake and fire, and had been built up again, but no phenomenon of Nature could be so terrible as was that destruction. Now it was being pulverized by titanic explosions, fused by mighty heat rays, and disintegrated by the awful force of the cathode rays. We can think only of that chaos of slashing, searing heat rays, the burning violet of pencil-like cathode rays, and the frightful explosions of the atomic bombs. It took them just sixteen minutes to destroy that city as no city has been destroyed in all the history of the Earth. Only the spot in the Nevada desert where the last battle was fought was to be more frightfully torn. But in all that city of the dead there was none of the suffering that had accompanied the other destruction; there were none to suffer; it was complete, instantaneous. Death itself is kind, but the way to death is thorny, and only those who pass quickly, as did these, find it a happy passing.

And then for perhaps a half hour more the great ships hung high above the still glowing ruins, supported on those blazing globes of ionized air. Then suddenly the entire fleet, in perfect formation, turned and glided majestically southward. The thousands of people of Los Angeles went mad when this news reached them. All seemed bent on escaping from the city at the same time, and many escaped by death. It took the Martians twelve minutes to reach Los

Angeles, and then the mighty shadows of their hulls were spread over the packed streets, over the thousands of people that struggled to leave.

But the Martians did not destroy that city. For two hours they hung motionless above, then glided slowly on.

# CHAPTER FIVE

ALL that day they hung over the state of California, moving from point to point with such apparently definite intention, it seemed they must be investigating some already known land. No more damage did they do unless they were molested. But wherever a gun spoke, a stabbing beam of heat reached down, caressed the spot, and left only a smoking, glowing pit of molten rock. A bombing plane that had climbed high in anticipation of their coming landed a great bomb directly on the back of one of the great ships. The explosion caused the mighty machine to stagger, but the tough wall was merely dented. An instant later there was a second explosion as the remaining bombs and the gasoline of the plane were set off by a pencil of glowing cathode rays. But when no resistance was offered, the Martian fleet soared smoothly overhead, oblivious of man, till at last they turned and started once more for the landing place in Nevada.

The last work on the projectors had been finished by noon that day, and they were installed in the ship immediately. Then came the test.

Again the *Terrestrian* floated lightly in the air outside the hangar, and again the pile of ingots leaped into the air to hang motionless, suspended by the gravity beam. Then came another beam, a beam of pale violet light that reached down to touch the bars with a caressing bath of violet radiance—a moment they glowed thus, then their hard outlines seemed to soften, to melt away, as still glowing, they expanded, grew larger. Inside of ten seconds the ingots of tungsten, each weighing over two hundred pounds, were gone. They had gone as a vapor of individual crystals; so gone that no eye could see them! The ray was a complete success, and now as the *Terrestrian* returned to its place under Waterson's skilful guidance, the men felt a new confidence in their weapon! The projectors of the disintegration ray had not yet been fitted with the polished iridium shields, and without these they would be vulnerable to heat rays.

It was during the installation of these that the accident happened. Wright had already put the left front projector shield in place, and was beginning on the right, but the small ladder from which he worked rested against the polished iridium surface of the car, and as this was rounded, he did not have a very secure perch. The shield weighed close to a hundred pounds, for iridium is the heaviest known metal, and it was constructed of inch-thick plates. While trying to swing one of these heavy shields into place, the changed direction of the force on the ladder caused it to slip, and a moment later Wright had fallen to the floor.

The heavy shield had landed beneath him, and his weight falling on top, had broken his right arm. Wright would be unable to operate any of the mechanism of the *Terrestrian,* which required all eyes, arms, and legs to work successfully. While Waterson installed the remaining shields, Gale hurried Wright to the nearest town in Waterson's monoplane.

It was three-thirty by the time he returned, and Waterson had mounted the shields. His great strength and size made the task far easier for him, and the work had been completed, and the shields finally polished, and welded in place.

The entire afternoon the radio had been bringing constant reports of the progress of the Martians. As they were doing no damage now, and were over a densely populated district, where any battle such as would result should the *Terrestrian* attack them would surely destroy a considerable amount of valuable property, Waterson decided to wait till they had left California. To the west was the ocean, and a conflict there would do no damage. To the east was the desert, and to the south was the sparsely settled regions of low property value. Only to the north would the value of the property be prohibitive to a final encounter.

When, at about five, news came that the Martians were returning to the desert landing spot in Nevada, Waterson at once set out to intercept them, and as his tiny car was prepared and waiting, the Martian armada came in sight, at first mere glistening points far off across the purple desert hills, but approaching hundreds of miles an hour.

Yet it seemed hours while those glowing points neared, grew, and became giant ships, though still miles away. When at last the leader of the Martian fleet came within about a half mile of its tiny opponent, without slowing its rapid flight, there sprang from its nose a glowing violet beam that reached out like a glowing finger of death to touch the machine ahead. But that machine was strongly charged with a tremendous negative potential, and the cathode ray was deflected and passed harmless, far to one side.

And now the *Terrestrian* went into action, retreating before the bull-like rush of its mighty opponents. The twenty great ships were drawn up in a perfect line formation, a semicircle, that each might be able to use its weapons with the greatest effect without interfering with its neighbor. Now from the gleaming *Terrestrian* ahead there sprang out a dull red beam, a beam that reached out to touch and caress the advancing ships. Six mighty ships it touched, and those six mighty ships continued their bull rush without control, spreading consternation in the ordered rank, for in each the pilot room had instantly become a mass of flame and glowing metal under the influence of the heat ray. The other fourteen ships had swerved at once, diving wildly lest that beam of red death reach them, but three great hulks dived, and in a dive that ended in flaming wreckage on the packed sands, ten miles below. The other three ships that had felt that deadly ray regained control before touching the earth, but those three that went down, mighty cathode rays streaming, struck and formed great craters in the sand.

BUT again that ray of death stabbed out, for one Martian had incautiously exposed his control room, and in an instant it too was diving. The mighty ray tubes forcing it on, it plunged headlong, with ever-greater velocity to the packed sands below. An instant later there was a titanic concussion, an explosion that made the mighty Martians rock, and stagger drunkenly as the blast of air rushed up, and a great crater, a full half-mile across, yawned in the earth's surface. Every atomic bomb in that ship had gone off!

The three ships that had been rayed retreated now and left thirteen active ships to attack the *Terrestrian*. The shield had been placed long before, and now as the Martians concentrated their heat rays on the glistening point before them, it was unaffected. While they were practically blind, they could not risk an exposure to that heat ray.

"Steve, I thought that heat ray was entirely cut out by the heat eliminator. How is it I could see your beam?"

"You can't see heat anyhow—and it does cut out all the infrared rays. The reason you can see that beam is that I send a bit of red light with it so I can aim it."

Again the Martians had drawn up into a semicircle, with the *Terrestrian* at the centre, and now there suddenly appeared at the bow of each a flash of violet light. At the same instant the ship before them shot straight up with a terrific acceleration—and it was well it did! Almost immediately there was an explosion that made even the gargantuan Martian ships reel, though they were over ten miles from the spot where the explosion occurred.

"Nice—they use a potassium salt in their explosive, Dave. See the purple color of the cannon flame?"

"Yes, but why not use the atomic energy to drive the shells as well as to explode them?"

"They couldn't make a cannon stand that explosion—but move—he's trying to crash us."

The Martians seemed intent on ramming the tiny ship that floated so unperturbed before them. Now three great ships were coming at them. Suddenly there was a sharp rattle of the machine gun, then as that stopped, the *Terrestrian* shot away, backed away from the Martians at a terrific speed. Gale had never seen the explosive bullets work, and now when the three leading Martian ships seemed suddenly, quietly, to leap into a thousand ragged pieces, giant masses of metal that flew off from, the ruptured ship at terrific speed, and with force that made them crash through the thick walls of their sister ship, it seemed magic. Those great ships seemed irresistible. Then suddenly they flew into a thousand great pieces. But all was quiet. No mighty concussion sounded. Only the slight flash of light as the ships split open. Titanic ships had been there—a deadly menace that came crashing down at them—then they were not there! And more, another ship had been crushed by a great flying piece of metal. Only the fact that these three had been well in front of the rest had saved the main part of the Martian fleet. The atomic generators of the one ship must have been utterly destroyed, for the great, glowing spheres of ionized air that showed the cathode rays to be working, had died, and the great ship was settling, still on an even keel, held upright by the gyroscopes that stabilized it, but falling, falling ever faster and faster to the earth, over twelve miles below.

"Steve—did—did I do that? Why didn't I hear the explosion?"

"You sure did, Dave, and made a fine job of it—three hits out of three shots—in fact four hits with three shots. The sound of the explosion can travel through air, but we are in free space."

But nine ships still remained active of the original twenty of the Martian Armada, and these nine seemed bent on an immediate end to this battle. This tiny thing was deadly!

Deadly beyond their wildest dreams—if it continued to operate, they wouldn't survive—it must be destroyed.

Again they attacked, but now the cathode rays were streaming before them, a great shield of flaming blue light. Again the thin red beam of death reached out, caressed the ships—and the pilot room became a mass of flames. But they had learned that the ships were controlled from some other part; they were coming smoothly on! Again came the sputtering pop of the machine gun. But it, too, seemed useless—the mighty explosions occurred far from their goal—the cathode rays were setting off the shells. And now one of the nine left the rank and shot at the *Terrestrian* with a sudden burst of speed. On it came at a terrific speed—one mile-three quarters-a half—

THEN there came a new ray from the bow of the tiny glistening ship. It seemed a tiny cathode ray, as it glowed blue in the ionized air, but, like the ship, it was strangely an iridescent violet—and as it touched the hurtling Martian, the great ship glowed violet, the color seemed to spread and flow over it, then it stopped. The ship was no longer glowing— and the strange ray ceased. But where the titanic, hurtling ship had been a moment before, was a slight clouding—and a few solid specks—small—the ship was utterly destroyed!

The other Martians withdrew. Here was something they could not understand. Heat they knew—explosions they knew—but this dissolution of a titanic ship—thousands of tons of matter—and in a fraction of a second—it was new; it seemed incredible.

But now again they formed themselves—this time they made a mighty cube, the eight ships, each at one corner—and five miles on a side the mighty cube advanced, till the *Terrestrian* formed a center to it. Now the great ships slowly closed in—but still the glistening ship remained in the center.

There was plenty of room to escape—then suddenly, as the cube contracted to a three-mile side, it moved. Instantly there came from all the great ships around it, a low but tremendously powerful hum—such a hum as one could hear around a power sub-station in the old days—the hum of transformers—and the tiny ship suddenly stopped—then reversed, shot back to the center of that mighty cube, and hung there! Now swiftly the cube was contracting—and still the tiny car hung there! It was jerking—but it moved only a few hundred feet each time—then suddenly it started—went faster—faster—then there was a distinct jar as it slowed down—almost reversed—but again it continued. At last it shot outside the wall of that cube and shot away with a terrific acceleration.

"Whew—Dave, they almost got us that time! That was a stunt I had never thought of—though I can see how it is done. They have tremendously powerful alternating current magnets on each of those ships. This car is non-magnetic, but a conductor, so there are induced in it powerful currents. You notice how hot it has grown in here—you can scarcely breathe—they induced terrific currents in our outer as well as in our inner shell. The result was that we were repelled from the powerful magnets. They were placed at the corners of a cube, so the only place that we could stay in equilibrium was in the exact center. When I tried to escape, I had to go nearer one of the poles, and the repelling force became greater. Then the ships on the far side shut off their magnets, so that they no longer repelled me—and I started to fall back—but I was able to pull out. The terrific acceleration I got just after leaving the cube was due to the repulsion of their magnets. You see it was very sizable! Had I had atomic energy only, I would never have gotten out of that field of force. I can, because of my material energy, escape every time. See—they are going to try again—let them—when they get close, we can turn on the disintegration and pick off the top ships. Then the bottom ships!"

Again the *Terrestrian* was held in that titanic field of force—that field was so great that all magnetic compasses all over the Earth were deflected, and the currents induced in the telephone lines, telegraph lines, power transformers, and all other apparatus were so great that many lines in the vicinity were melted. The cube contracted to a mile dimension before the glowing, iridescent ray of death reached out to dissolve that first ship—then a second—a third—a fourth—and the Martians were in the wildest confusion—the cathode rays prevented the *Terrestrian's* bombs from striking, but it also made their own projectiles useless. They had been sent to conquer this new planet for their race and they were failing. They could not rush that tiny ship—for the deadly disintegration ray would only destroy their ship before they had had a chance to crash into the *Terrestrian*. It seemed hopeless, but they tried once more.

Now from every side the ships of the Martians came at their tiny opponent, mighty hurtling hulks of hundreds of thousands of tons—it seemed they must get that tiny ship—there seemed no opening. The three damaged ships had joined in this last attempt—and as the seven gargantuan ships charged down at the *Terrestrian,* there sprang from it again the pale beam of disintegration—and one of the four remaining undamaged ships ceased to exist. The gap was closed—another ship was gone—and a third flashed into nothingness as the tiny opponent swung that deadly beam—then it was free—and turning to meet the four remaining Martians.

But now they turned—and started up—up—up. They were leaving Earth! And now, as the blazing sun sank below the far horizon of distant purple hills, one faltered, the burning violet spheres went dark, and it plunged faster and faster into the darkness below—down from the glowing light of the ruddy sun into the deep shadow far below—down to the shadow of Death—for the damaged generators had failed. And as that last great ship crashed on the far sands, the violet globes of light of the others were dying in the rare air far from Earth. The Martians had come, had seen, and had been conquered!

# CHAPTER SIX

"Steve—they are going—we have won. This planet is ours now—man has proven it. But they may bring reinforcements—are you going to let them go?"

"No, Dave, I have one more thing I want to do. I want to give an object lesson."

The tiny ship set off in the wake of the defeated giants— faster and faster. It was overhauling them—and at last it did—just beyond the orbit of the Moon. The undamaged ship was leading the train of four ships as they went back. Their world must have been watching—must have seen that battle—must have known. And now they were returning.

As the tiny ship came up to them the Martians turned at bay it seemed—and waited. Then from the tiny ship before them there came a new ray—invisible here in space—but a ray that caught and pulled the great ship it touched—the undamaged ship. In an instant it was falling toward the *Terrestrian*—then its great cathode tubes were turned on— invisible here in space also. Now it stopped, started away— but greater and greater became the force on it. It was a colossal tug of war! The giant seemed an easy victor—but the giant had the forces of atoms—and the smaller had the energy of matter to drive against it. It was a battle of Titanic forces, with space itself the battleground, and the great ship of the Martians was pulling, not against the small ship, but against space itself, for the equalizing space distorting apparatus took all tension from the *Terrestrian* itself. The great cathode ray tubes were working at full power now, yet still, inexorably, the Martian was following the *Terrestrian!*

Faster they were going now—accelerating—despite the mighty cathode rays of the Martians!

Of that awful trip through space and the terrible moments we had in the depths of space, you know. At times it seemed we must annihilate our giant prisoner, but always Waterson's skilful dodging avoided the bull rushes of the Martian, who would strain back with all available tubes, then suddenly turn all his force the other way—try to crash into us. It was a terrible trip—but toward the end he had decided to follow—and came smoothly. The strain of expecting some treachery kept us in suspense. Two weeks that long trip to Venus took. Two of the most awful weeks of my life. But two weeks in which I learned to marvel at that ship—learned to wonder at the terrific and constantly changing tugs it received—terrific yanks to avoid the hurtling tons of the Martian. I thought it must surely weaken under that continued strain, but it held. We had to get whatever sleep we could in the chairs. No food could be cooked, the sudden jerks threw us in all directions when we least expected it—but at last we reached the hot, steaming planet. Glad I was to see it, too!

The *Terrestrian* left its giant prisoner there, and as it rose through the hot, moist air it rose in a blaze of glowing color, for every available projector on its tiny surface had been turned on as a light projector—it was a beautiful salute as we left, red, blue, orange, green—every color of the spectrum blazed as a great, glowing finger of colored light in the misty air.

It took us but three days to return—Waterson admitted he went at a rate that was really unsafe—he had to put in another charge in the fuel distributer—water—and it held nearly a pint, too.

When at last we reached Arizona again, Wright was there to greet us—and so were delegates of every nation. It was supposed to be a welcoming committee, but every one of the delegates had something to say about why the secret of material energy should really be given to his country.

Waterson refused to give out the secret of that energy though. He demanded that the nations scrap every instrument of war, and then meet in the first Terrestrial Congress and write laws that might apply material energy to the ends of man, not to the ending of man!

It seems strange, the persistence with which the governments of the world held fast to those old battleships and guns! They were hopelessly useless now, yet they would not agree to that term of the agreement! It required Waterson's famous ultimatum to bring action.

"To the Governments of the Earth:

"For centuries and millenniums man has had wars. One reason has been that he has had the tools of war. The tools of war are going to be abolished now. Every armored cruiser, battleship, destroyer, submarine, aircraft carrier, and all other types of war craft will be taken to the nearest port, and every gun, cannon or other weapon of more than one mile range loaded on those ships. They will then be taken to the nearest ocean, and sunk in water of a depth of at least one mile.

"In the first place the weapons would be useless. The ship I now have has shown that. There will be no economic loss as the type of power they use is now obsolete. The iron and other materials they contain can be produced directly by new methods that are simpler than salvaging that metal. They are, however, curiosities that the future will be interested in. The navy department of Japan will select the finest ship of each type from each of the navies of any other country, and I will then transport that ship to a selected spot well toward the center of the Sahara desert where they will be set up as museums of naval history.

"This is to be done within seven days, or the *Terrestrian* will do it more completely. It must be done for the good of our race, and at last there is a power that can get it done—the *Terrestrian!"*

Needless to say, it was done. We all know the result. No armies meant no national spirit—no race jealousies can exist unless there is someone to stir them up, and now it is to the benefit of no one to do so!

The laws that made possible the application of Waterson's new energies are well known—and this manuscript is not the place for quotation of international and interplanetary law. It was a great problem, and we must acknowledge the aid of the Martians in solving it. Their experience in the application of atomic energy was immensely valuable. The light beam communication that Waterson made possible has done as much for us as have the energies he released.

And the peace that exists between these two races must always exist, for they are the only neighbors Earth can ever have. And they did not damage us much. We still feel a bit of dread of them I suppose, but statistics have shown that the trouble man himself caused in his wild panics did far more damage than did the Martian heat rays.

May God help these twin races, so close both in bodily form and place of birth, to climb on in friendly rivalry toward better things through the eons, as long as our sun can yet support life on the globes that wheel around it, migrating from planet to planet as the race grows, and the planets cool, settling on them as the Martians have settled on Venus.

And thanks to Stephen Waterson's foresight and vision in establishing the Supreme Council of Solar System Scientists, we dare hope this may come true.

# Part Two:
## *The Metal Horde*

IT would seem lack of generalship that permitted them to be discovered so soon, for had we not picked up those signals from the ether we should not have received that warning that meant so much to us, and it might well have been that this system would have acquired a new population. For it would have needed but little to shift the balance the other way! Once I watched Steven Waterson save the civilization of the Earth, but now I saw him in a greater role, for it was he who made possible the defeat of the Sirians. But even had his brilliant mind succeeded in working out the problem of the de-activating field without the precious hours gained by that warning, many millions more would have died before they could have escaped from Mars.

I was in his laboratory at the time he received the messages from the System government telling the import of those strange tone-signals out there in space. I seem fated to be with that man every time some great event breaks on the System. I was with him when Dr. Downey announced his discovery of the secret of old age—or, better, its prevention. Waterson was forty-two now, in years, but in body he was still twenty-eight for it was late in 1947 that he had taken Dr. Downey's treatment.

Those strange tone-signals had been heard faintly for days, but it was not until July 8th, 1961, that they were located in space, and then man began to realize something of the message they might bear.

Waterson asked me to accompany him to the System Capital on Venus, and I was present at that first Cabinet meeting, and at each succeeding meeting. Again I was close to the facts—and again Waterson has asked me to write a chronicle of that terrible War.

It was not till the signals had definitely been located as originating far out in space that man began to take more than a mildly curious interest in them. They were coming from the Metal Horde that was even then sweeping across space at a thousand miles a second to the planets ahead.

Their goal of ages was in sight. Sixteen hundred years of ceaseless rushing flight had at last brought them near.

When our ancestors were beginning to grumble under their Roman lords, in the time of Horlak San, when his mighty armies were sweeping their way across Mars under the newly developed heat rays, spreading death and civilization at one time, that menace started on its expedition.

When the Normans invaded England, when the mighty empire that the San dynasty had maintained over all Mars was crumbling, that journey was half done.

When Columbus first set foot on the shores of America, when Koral Nas formed the great union of the federated nations of Mars, that trip was three-quarters done.

But it was seven-eighths completed when Mars developed the first crude atomic engines, and when Priestly of England discovered oxygen. And during the two centuries of flight that remained before they reached their goal, there developed on those tiny planets the instruments that were to throw that mighty force down to defeat.

But I am to tell you of that war as I saw it; we have all seen it—all too closely! It was really but a little more than a month that that Menace of Metal hung over us there on Mars, but to us it seemed years, except to the frantically working scientists, striving desperately to discover some weapon to defeat them,

David Gale.

# CHAPTER ONE

A TINY glistening mote in space it was, as it sped toward the shining planet before it—the rapid flight of the car aided by the gravity of Venus. The call had been urgent, and the Earth had been in superior conjunction, that meant a full twenty-hour trip, even at 1000 miles a second, but now they were approaching the planet and the pilot was losing speed as rapidly as possible. There was a limit to what he could stand, though, and it took him many thousands of miles to bring the machine down to a speed compatible with atmospheric conditions of the planet.

The air of the planet seemed thick with traffic, mighty half-million ton lift freighters and passenger ships setting out toward Earth, smaller private machines, but none were slower nor faster than the others, for all were limited only by the acceleration they could stand. There was only one speed limit, that of economical, safe operation, for with all space to move in, there was no need of speed laws. Yet it seemed impossible to make any more than two thousand miles an hour through this slow moving air traffic—then there shone a little emblem on the bow of the little iridescent metal ship, and a huge freighter swerved respectfully aside. As by magic a lane opened through the thick traffic as the sign of the System President shone out.

The little ship darted along the ground a short way, then rose vertically, only to settle lightly on the roof of the great System Capitol. Two men came out and walked quickly to the elevator entrance, where three guards, armed with disintegration ray projectors, greeted them with a stiffly military salute. The larger of the men responded with a smile, and a brief salutation in the common language of the System, for these great men were Martians, each well over eight feet tall. They entered the lift, and quickly sank down one hundred and fifty stories to the Governmental Offices. They proceeded directly to the great Cabinet chamber, down through the long halls, lined on each side by huge murals depicting scenes in the history of the three planets. Then they came to the cabinet room and entered.

Thirty-nine men were seated there now, but as the two entered, they rose, and waited for the President to be seated. The forty greatest living men were in that room that day and all worked together, for they were scientists who had learned the value of cooperation. There was no rivalry, for each was the greatest in his own field and had no aspirations toward any other branch of science. And none but conceded the power of the Presidency gladly to the greatest of them, Steven Waterson of Earth.

"Gentlemen of the Cabinet, I am beginning to believe it is time we had something added to the Constitution forbidding Members of the Cabinet to rise on the entry of the President." Waterson deeply appreciated that compliment, as they all knew, but he could not feel at home in an atmosphere of diffidence. He was a scientist, a planner, not a diplomat. "I am sorry I was forced to make you gentlemen wait for me, but as you see," he continued, pointing to the great map of the System on the ceiling of the Cabinet chamber, where the slow motion of the planets in their orbits was being accurately traced, "Earth is in superior conjunction at present, and I could not make better time.

"I see from this memorandum that has been prepared for me that Mansol Korac, Martian Astro-physicist, is to be our first speaker. I take it you have had no official discussion as yet?"

He was correct in this assumption for the men had convened shortly before at his radio announcement that he would land within an hour.

Some years before there had been some agitation to have the Cabinet meetings carried on by Radio-vision plates, but the low speed of light had made the speeches a terrible failure, as they would frequently have to wait ten or even fifteen minutes while the radio messages were reaching them. Over short distances that method was practicable, but between planets light is too slow, it cannot be used.

"Some time ago our radio engineers developed a new instrument for detecting exceptionally short waves. They really came under the category of the longer heat radiations, but were detected electrically. While experimenting with this device they have been consistently picking up signals apparently originating in free space. At first these signals were exceedingly weak, but their intensity has grown uniformly and rapidly, and from the results some amazing conclusions have been drawn.

"They are originating at some source or sources out in space in the direction of the sun Sirius. I was asked to help the radiation engineers under Horus Mal in the calculation of the Astro-physical aspect of the problem. I believe that there are some man-made vehicles out there in space sending those signals. No man of the System has ever had reason to venture beyond the orbit of Neptune for any great distance; there would be no reason for it, as none of the outer planets are habitable. The rate of increase of the signal strength, coupled with observations made from Earth, Mars, and Venus, have made it evident that they are at present about one and a quarter billion miles away, but approaching us at the rate of 1000 miles a second. This means that in approximately two weeks they will reach our planets.

"AS to their point of origin we can only make guesses really. They are coming toward us with Sirius—and thousands of other stars—at their back. Of all, Sirius is the nearest, being approximately nine light years away. This means that they must have spent at least 1600 years on that trip across space. Dr. James Downey of Earth has recently shown us how to lengthen life almost indefinitely, so the problem of old age need not be considered. A supply of air and water would, of course, be no great problem with the Waterson apparatus for electrolyzing CO back to carbon and oxygen, using atomic energy fuel. Water, of course, is merely transmuted and recombined and thus automatically purified for use. A sufficient reserve of very dense materials could easily be carried that would make up for any losses by transmutation to the necessary gases. As yet we have not been able to make foods from energy, carbon, and oxygen and hydrogen, but I believe you, Dr. Lange, have made very considerable progress along that line, have you not?"

"I intended announcing at this meeting," said Dr. Lange, "the development of a commercial method of manufacturing any one of the sugars and several proteins directly from rock or water, by a transmutation and building-up process. The method has been developed."

"Then," continued the Martian, "there would be no need of carrying any great amount of food. That problem is settled.

"As there would be no resistance encountered in space, once the machine had been accelerated to its definite speed of 1000 miles per second, on leaving Sirius it would be able to make the trip across space with no expenditure of energy, until it reached its goal and slowed down to the speed of a planet. Hence no great amount of matter-fuel would be needed to drive the machine.

"But the problem of heating seems to me to be insoluble. In interplanetary space we have the radiations of the sun to depend upon, and they are decidedly sufficient, usually superfluously so.  But in the infinite depths of interstellar space, there is only darkness and a perfect reservoir for radiations.  There would be continuous cooling by radiation, and no sun to warm the ship.  I could understand how the ship might carry enough matter to warm it for one hundred years, but in sixteen hundred years so much energy must be radiated that the entire mass would not suffice.  Nothing short of an entire planet would be sufficient.  Polished walls would reduce the radiation, but still it would be too high.  I cannot understand it—unless these men can endure a temperature of but twenty or thirty degrees above absolute zero—then they could make it quite readily—but two hundred and forty degrees below zero Centigrade means that air—nearly everything would be solid, except a few rare gases.  No it seems impossible—yet we have the evidence!  I cannot understand how they have made this terrible migration, but I know that there are many different units.  I believe two thousand or more was the number you mentioned Horus Mal?"

"There seem to be a very considerable number of separate signals that we can distinguish.  I consider the two thousand a very conservative estimate," replied Horus Mal, the Martian radiation engineer.

"Then," continued Mansol Korac, "we must decide on some plan of meeting them."

The Martian sat down and for some time there was silence in the great hall.  At last President Waterson rose slowly to his feet.  His face showed his concern.  In times of emergency he always felt that these men here were responsible for the welfare of the twenty billions of human beings they controlled. And he was their leader, and therefore the responsibility was his.

"Mansol Korac, could you point out to us the approximate location of the approaching ships?" asked Waterson and handed him a small hand light and pointed to the great map of the system above them.

"I cannot be very exact, Mr. President; I do not know their location very definitely, but I should say about here, proceeding thus," The dazzling beam of white light stabbed up to the ceiling high above, and a sharp circle of light afoot across appeared; just within the orbit of Uranus, but well beyond Saturn. Then it slowly moved inward toward tiny glowing Mars. They were within the Solar System, but had not yet reached the Inner Ring of planets. Doubtless they who could make a trip across the great Void had the energy of matter at their disposal, and probably the disintegration ray. They would have no difficulty with the planetoids; they could merely beam them out of existence if they came too near.

The light snapped out, and each member of the cabinet turned toward Waterson again.

"Gentlemen, we see that they are within the Solar System already and appear to be heading directly for the Inner Ring, and Mars in particular. I do not know whether they come in peace or as invaders, but I think I can reasonably say that they are probably invaders. We all agree that they have made a trip of some 1600 years' duration. We all recognize the difficulty of such a trip. There are over two thousand ships in their fleet. I would not send so large a fleet to investigate the Outer Ring, but to send that great number of ships on a mere exploration trip of 1600 years—I do not think it is consistent. Then, too, we must allow them a life span of over three thousand years if we are going to admit that this fleet is for exploration, for it would be three thousand two hundred years before they could bring back news of their trip. In the meantime they might well have been wiped out by some stellar catastrophe, or they might have developed means of seeing us directly in nine years, the time light takes for the trip. Much as we would prefer peace, I fear we must prepare for war. But we can always go out to meet them peacefully, in a great battle fleet. That might convince them that it is better to deal peaceably with us and it would at least be a protection. I suggest that we have a discussion on this, and take a vote."

But there was no discussion, and the vote was unanimous, for the President's suggestion was the logical thing. They had to be prepared for either peace or war.

Then came the discussion of weapons. There was pitifully little to discuss. The interplanetary patrol fleet was a mere police force, designed to destroy meteors, turn comets or asteroids. There was no real naval fleet. But mechanical devices had reached a great peak of perfection and the little spaceships were so cheap, so easily operated, and so eminently safe, that nearly every family had several, and new ones were always in demand. There were mighty factories to meet this demand. Twenty billion people can absorb a tremendous number of machines. That was the greatest protection we had, and it was that quantity production, developed by the American, Ford, that made Waterson's campaign possible. But we were to learn much of quantity production methods before that war was over!

ORDERS were issued that evening to all the great factories over all three planets to begin work on a great quantity of ten-man-high speed ships. They were to be arranged with mountings for machine guns firing explosive bullets loaded with material explosive, each one equal to 100 tons of the old-fashioned Dynamite, with special mountings for Dis ray machines. The disintegration ray machinery was to be built by the companies employed ordinarily in making private power plants, hand lights, and the jumping belts. These belts had small projectors that threw a directional beam of force that tended to deform the curvature of space, at that point, and the result was a force that pulled the projector forward, for the space before it acted like a spring. If a magnet be held near a steel watch spring, the spring will bend, but it will try to straighten out and pull the magnet forward. If the magnet could pass through the spring it would progress, as the space curver apparatus was pulled through space. This was the principle of every ship now built, from these tiny two-kilogram (nearly five pounds) machines capable of lifting a man into the air, to the titanic new passenger-freight liners carrying as high as three quarters of a million tons.

The principle of the disintegration ray was not greatly different, and so the machines designed for turning these out in quantities were used to make the Dis ray apparatus with no great changes.

The heat ray projectors were made in quantities for every purpose; they were used for cooking, for welding metals, for warming the home, for melting down cliffs to make way for a building or a tunnel for water, for heating the mighty spaceships, for anything to which heat might be applied to advantage. These would make very effective weapons but for the fact that heat rays could be reflected. They would bounce off the car of the enemy without doing any damage if it were polished, as no doubt it would be.

Great liners of space were requisitioned and fitted with Dis rays, and with mighty attractor beam apparatus that would grip and hold anything short of another liner. Each of the ten-man-cruisers had a smaller attractor beam by which they could grip an adversary and hold to his tail with the tenacious grip of a bulldog and yet not weary the pilot with violent movement. These ships were exceedingly powerful, and their speed was limited only by the accelerations the passengers could stand.

But all the scientists of the System were working desperately to design some new weapon, some new machine that was a little faster, a little more powerful; although with resistance in space and with the tremendous energies of matter at their disposal, there was little lack of power as far as the speed of the ships were concerned. Ten thousand times more powerful than the titanic energies of atoms, this energy had defeated the Martians that memorable day in May, 1947, and it was a full ten billion times more powerful than the energies of coal, of oil, of the fuels man had known before that day. But they needed a machine that could project the Dis ray farther. Twenty-five miles was the limit, beyond that the tremendous electrical field that was used to direct it must be built up to so high a voltage that there was no practical way of insulating it. They must be satisfied with the twenty-five mile range—but the scientists were working at increasing the range.

They had two weeks before the Sirians would reach Mars, and in those two weeks much was done. There was a very carefully laid out system in all notices; the absolute truth was laid before the public, but there was also laid before them the evidences of Man's power. There were no panics. This was no weird thing to them, the landing of a fleet from another world; it was as commonplace to them as the landing of a fleet from the other side of the ocean had been a generation ago. The element of the unfamiliar was gone, and with it had gone the element that produces panic, that reduces the efficiency of a nation or of a System.

New production machines had to be built, new designs worked out, new dies cut, but it was done with the quickness that a generation of mass production had made possible, it was not new to them, this change of design overnight.

It required most of those two precious weeks to get the great machines working once more at their tasks, but at last a steady stream of ten-man cruisers was being poured out, 5000 an hour, night and day, from the factories of three planets. But there was only one day to work before the Invaders would reach Mars, and the fleet was gathered, 120,000 ten-man ships, manned by the volunteers of three worlds.

But in the meantime Waterson had built for himself a ten-man ship with triple strength of walls, and triple power plant installation, and an extra energy generator. He was experimenting with it, no one knew on what.

At last the invaders were seen. Far out in their course the scouts had met them. Those scouts were destroyed, without provocation; they did not even have time to finish their reports, but we learned enough.

Mars was a deserted planet now. All its population had moved to the other worlds. Most of them moved to Earth, on the other side of the sun. Only the workers in the great factories remained. They were not compelled to. They were told of the danger of their position, but those factories could contribute 1500 ships an hour, and they were manned. The fleet had gathered on Mars, awaiting the news of the Sirians, when the report of the scouts was flashed across the ether.

They told of a great horde of metal ships, shining, iridescent, ranging in size from tiny darting machines, ten feet long by one and three-quarters in diameter (mere torpedoes) to great transport ships. And there was a single spherical ship. A great sphere that floated in the center of a bodyguard of the thousands of its followers. There were literally hundreds of thousands of the little torpedo-ships, a few dozen of the cargo ships, and a few ships that seemed more like scouts of some sort. But it was apparent that the little torpedo-ships were the real fighters—tiny ships that spun and turned and darted like an electron in ionized gas. It seemed impossible that a man could stand those sudden turns at several miles a second, but they watched them, and went into nothingness as the Dis ray reached out from those tiny ships and caressed their ships.

They, too, had Dis rays—it would be a terrible battle, for man had that same force, a force so deadly they had feared to use it in industry. But man had the advantage of numbers.

The men on the fleet who saw those television plates glowing with the story of what was taking place out there in space decided that those torpedo-ships must be guided by radio. If they were it would be a simple matter to wreck that system by using a powerful interference that would drown out the directing wave and make its ships unimaginable.

The System Capital was temporarily moved to the Waterson Laboratories on Earth. There the forty men had gathered around great television plates and were watching the battle of the scouts. They were not to go to that battlefront. The System needed them.

# CHAPTER TWO

IT was midnight on the part of Mars where the Sirians first struck. The fleet of the Solar System was massed there to meet them. They seemed headed for the mighty gleaming city of Metal, below. Dornalus, the second city of old Mars, was located there—and they seemed bent on reaching it. As the Sirians drew near they threw forward a great shield of the torpedo-ships; then the great generators on the Solarian fleet forced tremendous etheric currents into space, and waited to see the motions of the tiny ships become erratic, but they darted about as steadily, as easily as ever. These Sirians must be small men! And they must be from a massive world, a world that had accustomed them to great accelerations.

Below them the city was deserted except for vision projector machines that hummed steadily, automatically, from a thousand points. They were broadcasting the message to the worlds and to the commanding officers on the other side of Mars. These men had direct control of the battle. They could not control it from Earth, for radio waves travel too slowly. Twenty minutes each way the waves took and in forty minutes the battle was more than over. It lasted only fifteen minutes—minutes of terrific carnage!

As the two great fleets came into contact, the Solarians drove into the mass of tiny ships, their Dis rays flashing in every direction. They had one advantage in that they sprayed nine streams of death from each of their craft; but the torpedo-ships were so unbelievably fast that it was nearly impossible to hit them. And they seemed to have no compunction about raying one of their own ships if a more than equal amount of damage was inflicted on their enemies. Logical, no doubt, but how inhuman.

The sky above the city became a blazing hell of Dis rays, heat rays, and exploding shells. The explosives were not safe, for they threw great flying fragments that could pierce the wall of a ship and send it down. They damaged friend and foe alike.

The Solarian fleet had a solid projectile of a single giant crystal of copper that was immune to the Dis ray. It could penetrate the walls of a ship and bring it down. But the explosive bombs were more often than not exploded or merely disintegrated before they reached their goal. A crystal of any sort was immune to the Dis ray, but it was not a protection against it. There was no known way of deflecting the Dis ray except by that special electrical field that directed it, and that could not be made to surround a ship. The copper crystals were used mainly to destroy the Dis ray projectors of the enemy. They were fired at the faint glow, and with luck they would hit the machine and instantly wreck the projector. More than one machine disappeared as its own Dis ray projector, wrecked by the fifteen-inch copper crystal, suddenly spread in all directions.

The sphere and its escort of transports hung back, surrounded by a great number of the torpedo ships. They did not join in the fight.

And at last the Solarian fleet was recalled. It was not right that they should make such heavy sacrifices. The city must fall, and it would be easy to crush the Sirians with a larger fleet. At the rate of 5000 Solarian ships an hour, they might well do so in three days. So the Solarians left, and behind on the ground there were a few ships; a great number had been rayed into nothingness. The Sirians had won this first victory, but the Solarians could soon make up for this loss. They had twenty billions to back them up, and they had the resources of three planets. It seemed as though the invaders could not last long, but we had yet to learn the true meaning of mass production.

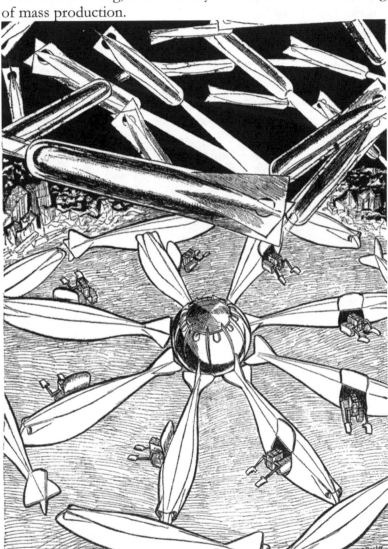

*Interior illustration by J.De Pauw*

No man could hang around the encampment of that alien race. But above them television broadcasts were suspended, and some were installed in the buildings of the city. But these were of no avail, for the Sirians seemed obsessed with the idea of making Mars a true sphere. They proceeded to level the great city with Dis rays. No news projector could remain there, of course, and several news projector men lost their lives. It was foolhardy to stay in that city; they had been forbidden, but nothing will keep a newsman out of a chance for a scoop. The projectors that hung above continued to show a weird scene.

The great sphere and its attendant transports sank gently to the ground and formed a great wheel, with the sphere as the hub and the transports as radiating spokes and the rim. High above them the darting torpedo-ships were wheeling in constant circles. It seems a miracle that not all of those news projectors were destroyed, but some did last till the early rays of the sun set them off as shining targets for the flashing Dis rays. It was a weird scene they showed!

Now from the sides of the great transports came, not men, but great machines, machines that lumbered along on caterpillar treads to set themselves down beside their parent ship, one from each ship, and proceeded to dig themselves in, about three feet deep. Then all seemed quiet, except for a steady hum from the great machines, fifty-eight in all there were, great machines—fully two hundred feet on a side. They worked there quietly now, and the men within them must have been totally covered, for they could not be seen. Apparently the Sirians dared not come out into the Martian atmosphere. And now something was happening that startled all the billions of watchers on the three planets. In the top of the great machines was a small trapdoor. Through this, there came a torpedo-ship that floated up a few feet, then darted off to join the wheeling machines above. Then eleven seconds later another came forth—another—each machine there was sending them out now. One by one those machines released a torpedo boat—one every eleven seconds, with the regularity of a clock.

At first men could not grasp the significance of this—but soon it became obvious. These wonderful machines were complete factories in themselves—portable, mass production factories for producing those torpedo-ships, and one each eleven seconds came from the end of the production line, complete. The noises there were no longer a gentle hum. There was a whir and rattle of machines. It was not loud, though considering the mighty works that must have been going on inside. But steadily now, that darting fleet of torpedo-ships was increasing the power, for all this work was obvious to these men who used similar processes in their work.

From the soil below them the machines dug masses of matter, and carrying it up into the machine transmuted its elements, into the elements necessary to their machines, then molded them, and automatically assembled them. It would require very little supervision, but that production rate was staggering! One each eleven seconds meant 325 completed machines an hour.

There were no signs of any men entering these ships, or the machines, so it seemed there must be some means of distant control that man knew nothing of, for it was improbable that all those men could have been in the parent machine from the beginning. No wonder the Sirians could lose these machines so freely. The ability to make them automatically from anything meant they cost practically nothing and could be produced in limitless quantity. The notion that Man was to be an easy victor was fast disappearing. These machines were coming to form an ever-growing cloud of wheeling ships. Still, man had destroyed fully half their fleet in that desperate struggle; they must spend some time in making up those losses. But Man had lost nearly a third of his great fleet. Four hundred thousand brave men had been lost. It was not even a victory, and it had cost Man far more than it had cost the Sirians. They had learned something from them, though. Perhaps radio control would enable man to do an equal amount of damage. Orders were put through to make an experimental fleet of thirty thousand radio-controlled machines.

IN the meantime a new thing was attracting the attention of the people on the planets. A new set of machines was issuing from the transports. These were smaller than the first set—low and squat—but they seemed far more flexible in their movement. They went off in an orderly line to a point a few miles distant from the main encampment and there formed themselves into two groups. One group remained still, but began to glow faintly, and a hum came to the televisors above. Then there began to flow from a spout on the side of each a steady stream of molten metal. This was poured into a somewhat similar arrangement on the other group, then these moved quickly away, and with their strange hand like appendages began to work quickly at a great rounded hull that was rapidly forming. The men watching understood. It was to be another cargo ship. Rapidly this hull grew under their swift manipulation, till it was completed in three and a half hours. An entire ship, except for the machinery, was completed. And now they began to work on another, and as they fell to work there started from the original cargo ships a long line of small, quick moving machines, machines that could run along the ground or drive through the air, and they were covered with arm-like appendages. Soon these reached the newly built hull, and quickly they were at work, getting material from the strange squat machines, entering the hull, and working at it. The second hull was nearly completed when one of the smaller machines flew back to the original encampment and went up to the sphere. From it, it drew a strange metal case, oblong, from which led a great heavy cable. This it carried back to the now completed ship and installed it somewhere inside. Then the ship rose easily from the ground and floated around a bit, landed again, and immediately there came out of it one of the torpedo-ship machines! None of these had gone in; it had been made by those slim, quick worker machines! And now there lumbered out a second machine—one of the strange hull maker machines—then two of the worker machines came out, where only one had gone in. The ship was complete, even to its strange crew! And now that strange crew was already at work, making others!

With the coming of dawn the televisors were rayed out of existence. But that evening more were installed, and every night during all the invasion there floated above them those noiseless televisors. They destroyed many, but many remained.

That night showed us a fleet of nearly a half million of the tiny torpedo-ships, and a rapidly growing cargo ship camp. There were more than a hundred now, for as each was completed, the machines made could aid in the more rapid construction of the next.

And that night they began their work of leveling Mars. That great fleet spread itself out over all the surface of Mars, and with flaming heat rays and the terrible Dis rays they cut down every remnant of the Martian hills. Twenty-four hours later the entire planet was one vast featureless plain. And on that plain there had been established eight camps. During this time the cargo ships had been moving, and during that twenty-four hours they did nothing. But Man was prepared. The radio-controlled fleet was ready to be given its first try.

The entire fleet was assembled above the surface of Mars, above that original camp, where still rested the one sphere. Then from far out in space the great control ships directed the dive of the radio-control-ships, making the distance one-twentieth part of a light second. The men directing the ships were no faster than that, could not respond sooner, and the greater distance gave them greater safety.

But now the radio-controlled ships were released, and permitted to drop, uncontrolled. They wished to give the Sirians no warning. Then when the ships were scarcely ten miles from the Sirian fleet, they were brought under control, headed nose down in a power dive, straight through the surprised upper layers of the fleet, and with Dis rays glowing they drove straight for the ships below.

Suddenly, there were great gashes in the ground beneath, and twenty of the cargo ships were gone in that first rush, and three more followed quickly. But while literally thousands of the Sirian torpedo-ships had been rayed, nearly half of the thirty thousand radio-controlled ships of Man were gone. And now they had to apply full power to prevent striking the ground.

But twenty-two of them continued on in straight fall toward the great sphere. They were rayed by a hundred ships before they could get really separated from their companions. And now the fast radio ships were destroying hundreds of the Sirians. They were formed in a vertical column reaching up ten miles, one above the other, with the nine Dis ray projectors going full blast and spinning as rapidly as was safe lest the machines fly apart due to centrifugal force, for the Dis ray will work practically instantaneously. The top ship was preventing the torpedo-ships' attack from above. Suddenly each of the ships stopped spinning; its Dis ray went out and they dropped like rocks. The radio control had been drowned out by powerful interference; they were no longer under the influence of the men, and they had ceased to function. The radio-controlled-ships would no longer be useful against the Sirians.

# CHAPTER THREE

NEARLY the entire fleet of the Sirian torpedo-ships had been wiped out by that spinning column. Now thousands of the manually controlled ships dove down at the weakened fleet. Everyone of the remaining ships shot up to meet the advancing fleet; there were still several thousand of the torpedo ships. And now the sphere rose with them, and among them. Suddenly the entire mass came together in the shape of a greater sphere with walls of torpedo-ships, and as it formed the torpedo ships snapped on their Dis rays, and started the entire surface of the sphere spinning! They seemed invulnerable in this formation, but they quickly moved away across the surface of the planet, the larger part of the Solarian fleet following, wondering what to do about it. It seemed impossible to attack the sphere of destruction.

But the cargo ships were left unprotected, and in a moment they had been beamed out of existence. The Sirians had lost many hours' work on this battle! And they lost more before the mighty fleet of torpedo-ships from the other camps rescued them. For now and then an explosive shell would penetrate the screen of disintegration rays. But within the outer shield was a second, virtually a shield of metal, for the metal sphere was surrounded by a solid mass of the torpedo-ships. But many of these were destroyed. More, too, were put out of commission by the copper crystals.

On the arrival of the great fleet from the other camps the tables were turned. The control ships had too low an acceleration, and there were too many ships for the ten-man machines to get, though they tried to make a screen of Dis rays that stopped the ships till they were rayed out of existence. Many of the control ships were lost and many of the ten-man ships.

It was then that Waterson announced two things that gave the Solarians new hope.

It was the fifth of August when the announcement was made. And it was the same day on which nearly the entire fleet from all the camps on Mars started off for Venus, but the movement was detected almost at once, and from great underground bases on Mars the Solarian fleet sent out fifty thousand ten-man ships. These ships skimmed along close to the ground, and their polished metal had been sprayed with a drab paint so that they seemed but shadows that became practically invisible as they sped along, widely separated, but rapidly converging on the site of the Sphere's camp. This had remained on Mars, guarded by so small a number of ships that it was evident they expected the Solarian fleet to go to Venus, as no doubt would have been necessary but for this swift counter raid.

So perfectly camouflaged were the Solarian ships that they got within ten miles of the camp without being discovered. Then, as their Dis rays flashed out, the entire group of the torpedo ships dove on them. There were nearly one hundred thousand of the ten-man ships, diving down at them in a zigzag course that made them impossible targets, but the fleet had been approaching from all sides, and now the entire Sirian defense was concentrating on the machines attacking from the north. Those from the south crept in behind them, and suddenly the sphere started into the air, then went flying out into space at terrific speed. It barely escaped the Dis rays of the attackers. Only its tremendous acceleration saved it. Now several thousand of the torpedo ships shot after it, the rest falling into the form of a great disc to block the path of the pursuers. Man had long been accustomed to two-dimensional maneuvering, but the ease with which these

Sirians fell into complex three-dimensional formations showed long practice in the art of warfare in space.

That raid was successful in that it forced the immediate return of the Sirian fleet, and very nearly destroyed the sphere. Over seventy-two thousand of the torpedo ships were destroyed, but we lost two thousand ships and twenty thousand men. But Waterson announced that the Sirians would no longer be able to escape because of their greater acceleration. He had discovered a method for using an attractor beam of a short range but considerable power to be used with an electro-magnetic device that would automatically turn on the instruments in such a way that no matter what the accelerations might be, no matter how great, as long as they were within the limits of the ship's strength, the accelerations and centrifugal forces would be instantly neutralized, thus making possible violent maneuvers that the sudden forces had hitherto made impossible. A demonstration of his new ship had confirmed it.

He took up a number of the Cabinet in his special machine, and turned hairpin turns at ten miles a second! The acceleration would have been instantaneously deadly had those neutralizers failed. They might as well have been under a half-million-ton freighter as it landed, as undergo those accelerations! But in that perfectly balanced room, it was not detectable.

The ship's hull was made triple strength, as were the power projectors, and the generators. It was powered like a freighter, and could reach its full speed of 1,000 miles per second at an acceleration 5,000 times that of Earth's gravity. Waterson, who weighed two hundred and ten pounds on Earth, would have weighed over five tons! It meant that the Solarian fleet would no longer be handicapped by the greater flexibility of the enemy ships. The plants that had been manufacturing the machines had already closed down temporarily, while the dies for these new machines were being made. But within thirty-six hours the first of the machines was being turned out.

And now a great crew of young men was being gathered to man them. They were all volunteers. There were to be one million ships, and that meant ten million men would be needed. Only modern methods could have made that possible, but with three populations, totaling over twenty billions, a sufficient number of volunteers came forward to make the work easy. As fast as these men came to the conscription stations, they were put into the new machines. And here also modern methods had helped.

The Waterson system of material energy release had been so successful, that the price of a completed car had dropped to well under one hundred dollars for the small two-man machines. And even for the interplanetary models not more than two thousand dollars needed to be paid, for the raw materials were absolutely free, the labor was mechanically reduced to almost nothing, and as the energy that drove these machines was as cheap as the raw materials, they merely charged enough to make the venture pay a decent return on investment and to pay the wages of the few machine supervisors and the office staff.

Men worked five days a week on three-hour shifts in the factories, but longer hours and more pay went to the builders, to the men who had to manually control the building construction machinery, for law forbade the building of offices on the mass production scheme, since that meant an unvaried, monotonous city. But everywhere wages were high, for wages depend, not on the amount of work men do, but on the amount of finished product they can turn out. The men accomplished more, and were paid more, but they worked less. It had taken many years to finally convince the Earth of that, but the example of American labor, with its shorter hours and higher wages was proof enough. And then the influence of the mighty energies Waterson had released made it even more apparent. Mars had already developed the system under the force of the released atomic energies.

High wages and cheap machines had meant that everyone owned one. And so absolutely safe were they that they commanded perfect confidence. This had been a big factor in the making of this mighty fleet. Everyone knew how to operate the machines, so it was easy to fill the places on the machines with pilots.

Nevertheless, special training was necessary to overcome the caution against quick turns that long experience had instilled in them all. Each accepted applicant was taken up in one of the new machines, and given a breath-taking ride—a ride that consisted in diving toward the Earth with terrific sudden acceleration. Then, just when the student felt certain they would crash and become a mass of molten metal, the ship was brought up, not a mile from the ground, to settle gently; then, when they almost touched the ground, they leapt into the air again with an acceleration that shot them out of the atmosphere with the velocity of a meteor, while the outer wall of tungsto-iridium alloy glowed cherry red. Then came sharp turns at ten or twenty miles a second, till at last the students no longer gripped the arms of their seats in anticipation of a sudden acceleration. Then they were taken down and given a ship to experiment with.

But none of these men had ever handled a weapon of the sort they were to use, so mimic battle practice was held, with the glowing rays of a harmless ionizing beam instead of the deadly Dis rays.

# CHAPTER FOUR

DAILY reports were coming from the Martian scouts as time went on. The Sirians, too, had decided to do some fleet building, for nearly three-quarters of their fleet had been destroyed. The production rate of man's factories, 120,000 a day, had gained a slight lead. It would require ten days before a fleet of a million could leave for Mars with a home guard of two-hundred thousand ships.

The destruction of the Martian plants had lowered the production rate to about 3,500 an hour, but shops put up rapidly on Earth and Venus had quickly brought the production-rate back, and it would be nearer 7,000 an hour by the time the last of the fleet had been finished.

The spinning sphere formation of the Sirians had been almost invulnerable, and an exceedingly destructive formation. The Solarians had chosen several thousand of their crack pilots to practice this maneuver, but despite almost constant practice during the entire ten days, it was a miserable failure as soon as they tried to progress. Standing motionless it was a very effective procedure, but the spinning column was decided on as more effective as long as they had no ship to protect. There were twenty groups that practiced that maneuver.

And then Waterson announced that an associate of his, working in his laboratory, had developed a method for using a triple electrical field to direct the Dis ray, making possible a ray with a range of over sixty miles. This would be absolutely fatal to the spinning sphere system of the Sirians. The Sirians very evidently did not know how to project the Dis ray any further than twenty-five miles. The ability to stand off and hit them would break down the sphere of Dis rays very quickly.

There was only one objection. The rays were very powerful, so powerful that they required triple power generators, but the special field of electrical force was the worst problem. The field could not be made sufficiently strong if a single layer of the force was used, but the invention of a method to back up the first with two other layers of equal voltage, thus getting nearly three times the effect without exceeding the capacity of the insulation, had made the new machine possible. This special field was produced by circularly moving cathode rays, or exceedingly high velocity electrons, and therefore could be produced only by atomic methods. This meant ten thousand times the amount of fuel a similarly powered material engine would have required, but material energy of course yields only wave motions of the transient or unstatic type, a type that cannot stand still. Atomic energy can yield static waves as well as unstatic; the electron can stand still, and is a perfect example of the stationary wave.

These limitations, in turn, meant that a tremendous weight of equipment was needed. And a corresponding great volume of space was required. In the end they had to use specially reinforced freighters to carry the great projectors, each of which could carry but two projectors. Due to their long range, however, the ships were at least self-protecting. There was not time to make and equip more than twenty-eight of these ships before the fleet was scheduled to start. They were completed ahead of time. Some of their trial trips more than fulfilled the best hopes of the inventor. Dr. William Carson, the physicist who developed it insisted that it was really Dr. Waterson's suggestions that made the thing possible.

We had learned something of spatial warfare formations from the Sirians. Now we were to learn a bit of the strategy of spatial warfare.

THE Solarian fleet sailed for Mars on the fifteenth of August, 1961. They were a scant twenty million miles from their goal when a report came from a scout that something was happening down in the Sirian camp. Almost immediately after that the Sirians flooded our entire system with so terrific a barrage of radio frequency static that communication was impossible. They could not transmit from Earth to Venus, and the communication was very poor even from one side of Earth to the other, despite the fact that over a half billion kilowatts were used. So intense was this barrage, that if two of the torpedo ships near the sending apparatus came within twenty or thirty feet of each other, great crashing sparks leapt across, and instantly they were fused. Scouts saw this happen twice.

The Solarian fleet continued on for Mars. They should cover the remaining distance—twenty million miles—in five hours by pressing the ships a little, although higher speeds made the rate of approach of asteroids so great that they frequently could not be detected before they collided with the ships.

Only two and a half hours later a scout came into sight at terrific speed. He must have been doing over two thousand a second, an exceedingly dangerous rate—but his acceleration neutralizer enabled him to slow down safely. He reported that the entire Sirian fleet had risen from Mars, leaving a very few machines behind—this time taking the sphere with them—and had set out for Earth!

Earth was on the other side of the Sun—a long two hundred and twenty million miles to go! The Sirians had a lead of three hours. They had as great a speed as the

Solarians and would reach Earth before the Solarians. But they would at least be delayed by the two hundred thousand ships—more now, for the steady production would have built the quota up to over six hundred thousand, or a million by the time they could return.

The Sirian fleet had been built up to nearly three million though, which could easily crush the fleet of a million, and the second million later—separately. The trip would take them sixty-two hours. Scouts had been sent ahead to Earth at a dangerously high speed to communicate the news, and the entire fleet had increased its speed to a rate that was considerably higher than safety warranted, but a continuous play of Dis rays was considered sufficient safety at fifteen hundred miles a second. The Sirian fleet had been reported to be making thirteen hundred and fifty, so the Solarians should pass them, or meet them, just shy of the Earth, where the other fleet would be waiting. They should have no difficulty to crush the Invaders with the two million ships.

The radio interference was being maintained by a ship anchored somewhere in space. It was no doubt well-protected, and to attack it successfully would have meant the loss of a large number of ships, for the time spent in the attack would delay them irreparably. They must continue to Earth.

There were no scouts from the Sirian fleet—yet there should have been, for over a thousand ships had been following them, far behind. None ever reached Earth to warn the fleet. Every one of them was destroyed. But when the Sirian fleet was well on its way—it turned—and headed *for Venus!* They had purposely let that one scout reach the Solarian fleet with the news that the fleet was headed for Earth—then they redirected their course. The scouts from the Solarian fleet did reach Earth—but soon after the last of the scouts following the Sirian fleet had been destroyed, their radio barrage was lifted. All the ships on Venus were concentrated on Earth, and Venus was left unprotected.

Twenty hours after the fleet had turned back, the radio barrage was again lowered over the System. It was ten hours later that the Sirians reached Venus.

While the radio barrage had been lifted, Waterson had had an idea that there should be some protection for the planet. It did not seem that the planet should be completely stripped of its defenses, and he had suggested that at every city great Dis ray machines of the sixty-mile range type be set up. His suggestion was followed, and at every city on Venus the great machines were installed. There were many of them now, for during the hundred hours the main fleet was in flight the new machines had been put on a quantity production basis.

But all the ships that were equipped with them were sent to the defense of the unattacked Earth! And it was those machines that prevented the landing of the Sirians. They came to the night side of the planet, of course, coming, from Mars. It would be thirty hours before they would be expected on Earth—thirty hours before the main fleet would reach the planet—and then there would be the 160,000,000-mile trip to Venus if they were to get there in time to rescue the planet.

But the Sirians could not approach within beaming distance of the cities, and all those that did try to do so, were brought down as a cloud of powdery dust. It was Waterson's caution that saved the billions of people on Venus.

But were they to be saved? The Sirians decided they must destroy the works and the people on Venus, so they made one desperate effort. They had at least sixty hours to work in, and now they had a plan that would require time. They retired some hundred miles from the planet, then the entire fleet, torpedo ships, cargo boats, and the entire bodyguard of the Sphere lined up, and then switched on powerful attractor beams. Immediately, the combined effect of over three million of these emanations took hold on the planet, and great tides began to rise in its mighty oceans. Many lives were lost in the seaside towns, when the tremendous waves rushed in over the land. But astronomers on the planet and most of the System's scientists were there to watch the Sirians on Mars through their great telescopes. And these astronomers saw what the Sirians intended, and saw that they were well on their way to fulfilling their aim.

# CHAPTER FIVE

A PLANET is balanced in its orbit about its parent sun with the delicacy of a diamond on a jeweler's scales. But, like the diamond, if it be displaced by some force, it reaches a new state of equilibrium. Thus, if the diamond is further lowered in the scale by adding a small weight, it soon reaches a new point of equilibrium. No conceivable force, therefore, could be great enough to displace the planet in its orbit more than a few million miles by pulling it either in toward the sun, or out from it, and as soon as that force was released, it would spring back to its original position as the diamond would regain its balance on removing the disturbing weight. For the sun pulls on a planet with a titanic force; it draws it in with the apparent force gravity, and another similar, but opposite force, centrifugal force of its revolution in its orbit, is constantly tending to throw it into the depths of space.

These are the two forces that are always balanced. Suppose the planet is drawn nearer the sun; it revolves in a smaller orbit—and it revolves in that smaller orbit with a higher speed—for it has fallen in toward the sun; it has gained speed as any falling body would. It has gained speed in the direction of the sun, but this has operated to increase its rotational speed. Thus it has gained a greater centrifugal force—you can see the effect with a bit of chalk on the end of a string. The smaller the circle it swings in, the greater the tendency to fly outward. But as long as we continue the force that was added to draw it in, it will remain in equilibrium. Remove this extra force and at once the planet will fall away from the sun, losing speed as it does so, till it has reached a point where it is once more in equilibrium with the force drawing it inward.

Now reverse the problem. Let us draw it away from the sun. Now the orbit is longer, and it has lost speed in moving from the sun. It cannot stay here; it is not in equilibrium, unless the force that drew it out is maintained. To free the planet from the sun, one would have to lift hundreds of quintillions of tons of rock through billions of miles, against the terrific gravity of the sun. It is too much.

Thus we see that as long as the planet revolves in its orbit, it will never fall, and to pull it away from the sun is impossible as long as it revolves in its orbit. But if it slows down in its flight about the sun it at once has less centrifugal force. It automatically falls toward the sun until it has gained velocity enough to establish a new orbit of equilibrium. If this energy, too, is withdrawn; if it is made to stand still in its orbit; it will fall straight to the sun. It is the only way such a thing might be done. And it would take the energies of matter, and strain that to the utmost, to accomplish it.

This was the plan of the Sirians. Three million ships were dragging like a titanic brake on the planet as it wheeled in its orbit, and slowly, steadily it was falling into the blazing furnace of the sun. Their ships were not designed for this task, but they could do it in the sixty hours at their disposal. In a short time Venus would be falling directly toward the sun, but it would take many hours for the seventy-million-mile fall. Even if it were stopped before it reached the sun, any place within twenty million miles would be unbearable.

It was the distressed planet itself that warned the people on Earth and the men of the fleet that the Sirians would never reach Earth, for the radio was still dead. But the fleet turned for Venus at once. They were far to one side of the path to Venus, and they would have to turn, but it would take them thirty, instead of sixty hours to reach Venus. And the other fleet was coming from Earth. They were not quite a million strong, but those machines that had been produced on Venus would come also, and that would bring the total numbers up to over a million, and with the main fleet the number would be well over two million. There were also three hundred of the long-range Dis ray ships now, for many more had been produced, and Venus would supply an equal number.

WE can only admire the wise action of the Commandant of the Venerean fleet, Mals Hotark, in not sending his pitiful fleet of a few thousand out to fight with the Sirians. The members wanted to, the people of Venus wanted him to, but he wisely waited until he saw the fleets of the System approaching. It would have done no good, and lost many lives, and valuable ships to have gone in advance to the attack.

Many people tried to leave Venus, but enough machines were freed of the task of stopping the orbital motion of the planet to patrol the heavens and keep the people from leaving. They beamed thousands of private cars out of existence; it seemed unnecessarily cruel.

The two great fleets were drawing nearer to the planet, converging, and at last they got so close that they could carry on a radio communication by using the terrific power of over two billion kilowatts of energy. The amount of power that Sirian machine was throwing off has been estimated at a minimum of fifty billion kilowatts. We know that enough power could be picked up from a hundred meter aerial on Earth to operate a small, high frequency motor.

When radio communication was established, they agreed to wait until they could join, for the fleet from Earth was two hours ahead of the main fleet. The loss of time was made up for in greater efficiency of action. They would need it all. At last they joined fleets, one mighty disc of two million airships, they flew on through space at a steady rate of five and three-quarter million miles an hour.  They arranged themselves in a mighty cone as they came nearer Venus.  Already the machines had slowed it down so greatly that the planet was over a million miles out of her orbit, and rapidly adding to this mileage.

But now as the great cone approached, the great ships with the long-range Dis rays leading, they were discovered.  The cone formation was chosen, for that is the three dimensional equivalent of the two dimensional V that man had used in war on earth for thousands of years.

Now began the greatest battle in the history of the System.  Here were two mighty forces slashing at each other with terrific disintegration rays, fighting in the great Void, and five million powerful ships darting around, slashing, stabbing with a death that struck with the quickness of light.

As the great cone of the main fleet attacked from one side, there was a smaller cone attacking the Sirians from the other, but long before the Sirians could bring their rays into effect the long-range rays had torn great holes in their ranks.  The Sphere had retired with its escort at once, going swiftly to Mars.  The main fleet was too busily engaged hi fighting the Sirians' main fleet to worry about the Sphere at present.

A dozen times the great spinning sphere formation was tried by the Sirians, but each time a withering blast of the long range Dis ray cut it up as a tool held against a spinning block of wood cuts it down in the lathe.

Their strongest formation was useless, and they could no longer outmaneuver the Solarians, the new ships could turn and dart as quickly as they, or even more quickly.  The big Dis ray ships were not equipped for fast fighting, so when there were none of the spinning sphere formations to break up, they retired to a safe distance, and waited for any ships that might attack them. Few did. It proved suicidal. But steadily the forces of man were conquering.

In a hell of flashing Dis rays, the new ships were proving their worth. The flaming rays had seared the land below for many miles, but the fleet of the Sirians was fast going. The new fast ships of man could dodge the rays of the Sirians, turn and dart on the tail of their attacker, then hang there, the attractor beam giving them an added grip until they could flash the machine into nothingness with the Dis ray. They turned, ducked, darted ahead with terrific speed, suddenly stopped, and then were going full speed again. And another Sirian ship was gone.

Now it was the delicate apparatus of the Sirians' ships that suffered; they could not keep up with the sudden turns of this flexible adversary. And their great fleet had been reduced to a scant quarter million, but we had lost nearly a half million ships, five million men, in that titanic struggle. Such a battle could not last long. It was impossible. Nothing could stand before the Dis rays, and with those turning, darting ships, sooner or later every ship must come under the influence of those rays. But now the last of the torpedo-ships were fleeing into space. But we did not care to have to fight them again—and they too were rayed out of being. They could no longer dart away from us before we could catch them—that was for us now!

But now the fleet returned to a greater task. Venus had been falling toward the sun, and was nearly a million and a quarter miles off and within her orbit. Now a great fleet of cargo carriers from Mars, Venus and Earth came up, and with them came wrecker ships, capable of picking up on their powerful attractor beams an entire million-ton passenger-freight liner—great liners themselves, all equipped with attractor beams. Soon they were all using their power to bring the planet back to its normal speed. It did not take the ships of that mighty fleet, many specially designed for heavy listing and towing, many designed for tremendous loads, very long to bring the planet back to its age-old orbit.

In former days we would have found a world wrecked by panic. But this later generation had learned to trust in the powers of the ships they had, and there had been little of the terrible panic that would have affected the world of a generation ago. Then, too, they knew that with the demonstrated power of the long-range Dis rays, they could safely convoy a fleet of the great passenger liners to safety.

What helped also was the fact that the human mind cannot grasp the full significance of the fall into the sun. If you were told that the planet you were on was sinking toward the sun, you would be surprised, horrified, and would probably try to make a bargain—buy on real estate, while the other man sold his to get his money out. You would simply fail to comprehend the magnitude of the catastrophe. It has never happened, and never will, the mind says, and we unconsciously believe it. Your neighbor would joke about it to you. Of course many would leave, but most people would stay till the actual physical heat of the sun drove them off. We are constituted that way.

But now the radio barrier was down, and news from the Martian scouts made men hesitate. The remaining cargo ships had settled on Mars and were even now pouring out their strange crews. But they were not building cargo ships. Everyone of the worker machines were kept in action constructing duplicates of themselves as rapidly as possible. Already a great number of them had been made—over seven hundred of the machines it was estimated—and now these were engaged in similar work. The number grew in a steady geometrical series.

But the scouts were driven away by the torpedo ships. Then there was no news of the operations until nightfall permitted the scouts to creep up and install the usual floating vision machines.

Then at last we understood the reason for this tremendous number of inoffensive worker machines. There was a great seething mass of metal around the workings now. Great blazing lights illuminated the scene as brightly as day. There was a great horde of shining metal machines working swiftly about the great plain. There seemed to be thousands of them now, and they were all busily at work on great machines—the torpedo-ship machines! There must have been nearly a thousand already completed and already the fleet that had escaped had been built up to many thousands by the rapidly working machines, and a steady stream of long glistening shapes rose—only to be lost in the darkness beyond. Steadily the great machines were being put together, and steadily the great fleet was being augmented.

Before morning that fleet had reached two hundred thousand, and was now growing at the rate of twenty-five thousand an hour. Steadily this rate was increasing. The fleet was too large to be attacked by man's weakened fleet, for the delay in putting Venus back in its orbit had given the Sirians a chance to build up an invulnerable fleet. The added time of the trip to Mars meant a still greater fleet. Already their production rate was far greater than Man's. Man could not hope to compete successfully. We were learning the meaning of quantity production.

Had it been possible to attack them with the long-range Dis rays it would have been tried, but the plan was hopeless. Before the fleet could reach them there would be 100,000,000 miles to go to reach them, and it would take approximately twenty hours, in which time, at the present rate of increase, the Sirian fleet would have reached a total of three million again. They would all concentrate their attack on the long-range Dis ray ships. No Solarian ships could help without interfering with the action of the Dis ray ships, and they would need help, for each ship carried only two beams. More could not be carried. They would merely be held at bay, unable to attack their goal, useful only in breaking up the spinning sphere formation, but that could be prevented.

The Solarians had learned that trick from the Sirians. The Sirians had succeeded in breaking up every spinning column formation by simply getting into the midst of it before it was formed completely. It required perfect coordination of several machines to do it, but it was always done. The long-range Dis rays were excellent now in defending a city, but useless for attack because of the terrific weight of the apparatus.

They could not attack the Sirian fleet. If they did the production machines would have been so built up by the time they reached the planet that any ordinary rate of destruction would be easily equaled by the production! Within three days it was decided that the Sirian fleet would be built up enough to attack. They would then attack our planets, no doubt.

# CHAPTER SIX

A CABINET meeting was called at the Waterson laboratories on Earth. There Waterson first demonstrated the weapon that finally conquered in the terrific struggle. Before the members, on the Cabinet table, was a small portable material energy disintegrator, a machine that gave off its energy as light. There was a second machine at the other end of the table, a machine that occupied about two cubic feet of space, and on one side of it was a small switch and a dial; on the other was a familiar looking projector.

Dr. Waterson spoke:

"Gentlemen of the Cabinet: I have here a new machine that my laboratory has developed. I will demonstrate its action first," The light was switched on, throwing a brilliant shaft of light against the ceiling. Then Waterson snapped on the switch of the new machine, and there appeared a strange beam of bluish, ionized air. But unlike any other known ionizing beam, it was shot through with streamers of red fire, long, hair-thin streamers that wavered and flickered in the blue tube of the ionized air. It reached out, touched the light generator, and passed on, through a series of plates of different materials. But the instant that strange beam struck the light-machine, it went out. Then a moment later, when the new machine was turned off, the light snapped back on.

"Gentlemen, this machine will produce a field, directional in this case, that will so modify the properties of space as to make it utterly impossible to disintegrate matter into energy.

"There is some tendency to fix energy as matter. I think that will be interesting to us in the event that this war is successfully concluded. But at present we are interested in the properties of the beam in that it will stop the disintegration of matter.

"The process depends on the modification of the properties of space. It is well known that in ordinary space, such as we know, there are twenty coefficients of curvature. In ordinary empty space, ten of these have zero values, and the ten principal coefficients have certain non-zero values.

"This machine so, affects space that it makes all the coefficients of space have non-zero values, and fixes these values to suit its own purposes. The results are amazing. I have done some things with this machine that makes me truly afraid. But we are interested in it because certain of the values we can assign operate to force space to take such curvatures, that any change of the condition of matter to condition of energy is impossible. On release of the ray, the space returns to its normal curvature.

"Working out the theory of this machine has been a tremendous task. Even the great calculating machine, the new integraph developed last year, and it is a far cry from that first one that M.I.T. developed in 1927, required many weeks of work to solve the problem in twenty coefficients of space. In so doing at one stage we had to assume a space of twenty dimensions in order that the correct values in the four true dimensions might be determined.

"But there is still a great deal of work to be done. We must develop practical machines of a range of many miles. There is no difficulty in using the ray, since, as it is a condition of space, not a vibration, it is impossible to stop it by any shield.

"There is only one way to work with it, to create it directionally. We make the field by projecting certain strains along a beam, then once started the field follows that line to a distance dependent on the strength of the generator.

"But this will require at least five days to get into working form. I suggest that in the meantime Venus makes several million of the long-range Dis ray projectors, and distribute them all over the planet, to be turned on from a central station, or by their own separate crews. I have no doubt that the Sirians will attack that planet before we are ready to attack them. Earth, too, must be prepared. But in the meantime we can begin the work on the new de-activating field projectors, as I call them."

Waterson was right. It was three days later that the Sirian fleet left for Venus with a number of torpedo ships so tremendous, it was absolutely inconceivable. There were over two hundred million of the ten-man machines! When they started to settle about Venus, the sky was so filled with them that it was literally dark for many miles. They attacked at Horacoles, the System Capital, but the fields of the great Dis rays were too much for them. Neither bombs nor Dis rays could reach through.

The air was dense and filled with artificial smoke to prevent the transmission of heat rays and great winds were created for the purpose of carrying the heat away; but this was done automatically by the expanding air before long. They could not attack the city. All over the face of the planet were the great Dis ray emplacements. Great ships hung even over the great rolling oceans, sending the blue rays of ionized air up like some column that was to hold the Sirians from the Planet. And they did.

But now again they began to slow down the planet—not gently as they had had to before—but rapidly. The planet would have been pulled to pieces, except that the very attractor beams that were pulling on it tended to relieve the stress. But the cargo ships of Venus were pulling to keep the planet in motion. It was a strange thing to contemplate! Two mighty forces, one a fleet of two hundred million small ships, the other a force of as many thousand huge freight carriers, having a tug-o-war for a planet!

But the odds were too great. Slowly the Sirians won. The planet was steadily dropping toward the sun. Now it seemed no fleet could come to aid them, and the Sirian fleet was being augmented constantly by a steady stream of ships from Mars. It was the sixth day after the announcement was made that Waterson had a fleet ready to attack the Sirians. The Venerians also had a fleet ready, prepared by the directions of Waterson's engineers sent by radio-television and radiophone. They were ready to attack, and the Terrestrian fleet arrived at Venus just six days after the announcement of the new weapon.

The practical projector of this new ray had been quite heavy, and they had been mounted in groups of twenty projectors on special hundred-man ships, using the same acceleration neutralizer used on the ten-man ships. They were arranged to throw a wide beam, so wide that the new ships with twenty, could prevent any action in a field of over two hundred miles depth, and in a cone with a base of six hundred miles diameter. The ships they had could approach within a hundred miles of the Sirian fleet, without being seen, for they were painted black, and therefore showed no lights. In the darkness of the void they were easily hidden.

THE entire expedition went as planned. The radio barrage had not been turned on, and they were in constant communication with the Venerians. The two fleets were to attack simultaneously, over different areas, so that between them they could wipe out so large a number of the enemy ships that the fleet of two million could easily handle the task.

Ridden in the utter dark of the void they crept up on the Sirians. They were in the sunlight, but the black coating kept them invisible, while the Sirian ships shone brilliantly. Then at last the tip of the great cone formation was within easy striking distance of the fleet.

There reached out the strange ray, and here in space it was utterly invisible. But suddenly the ships within its range began to waver, to fall together under mutual gravitation. With one swoop they all shot toward the ships in space that had paralyzed them, for the attractor beams had been turned on them. As the great mass of ships fell rapidly toward them, long-range Dis rays reached out, and they melted into clouds of shimmering dust. Great swaths were cut through their ranks.

A similar scene was taking place far to the left of the Terrestrian fleet where the Venerian fleet was working havoc among the invaders. Now the last of the ships had been rayed into nothingness and a great fleet of the Sirians was rushing forward to attack for the ships invisible on account of their black line had been electrostatically located now. But as the Sirians came within one hundred miles of the other fleets, the ships all ceased to accelerate, to change direction; they just drifted straight into that cone of Dis rays. All walls of the de-activating field were lined with the ten-man ships; their shorter-range Dis rays prevented any Sirians from escaping.

Bright lights shone out on the Solarian fleet now—they wanted the Sirians to attack. The original cone formation had shifted rapidly; now it was a double cone; then it changed to a quadruple cone. There were six hundred of the de-activator ships and these were arranged so that they shot their rays off in four directions, making four cones of de-activated space, with the fleet of deactivator ships at the apex. Thus they were protected on all sides, and quickly, as the Sirian fleet spread out, more ships rose and there were six cones branching out.

In the center rested the main mass of the fleet, the long-range Dis ships, their attractors pointing out into the cones to draw the disabled ships of the Sirians into the range of their Dis rays, emanating in thousands from the ships lining the sides of the de-activated cones of space. The fleet was invulnerable and so sudden and complete was the failure of their power in these de-activated regions, that they did not seem to have time to warn their fellows. Many millions of the ships were lost before the wild charge could be checked; then the six-cone formation entire began to move slowly around; the Sirians, waiting to see what was to happen, were caught before they were aware that they were in danger.

Many, too, were caught by the powerful attractor beams of the heavy ships within—drawn in by the greater power of the heavy ship, till their power failed. But at last the Sirians had learned the effective range of this new power and tried hard to avoid it. The six-cone formation was immediately broken up, and the six hundred de-activators went out individually, each followed by a swarm of the ten-man ships to disintegrate the ships caught in the de-activating cones.

The Terrestrian ships were marked by a blazing blue light, so that if they too were caught in the de-activating field, they were not disintegrated. Only those around them were, and they were then released, as the ray did not seem to have any injurious effects on man, except to give him strange dreams. In some way the brain was stimulated by the ray, as long as the ray was used.

The de-activator ships were completely self-protecting; they could stop any number of attackers from any direction, provided the paralyzed ships were disintegrated as soon as caught, for if too many were piled up, the tendency of the matter to disintegrate in the engines, plus the natural tendency of the space to resume the normal curvature, caused the ray to become ineffective as it was overpowered, and one ship was lost in this way.

Too many ships piled up, and only part of them could be rayed out by the ship itself, and there were not a sufficient number of helping ten-man ships. But the mighty fleet of the Sirians was already beaten. They still outnumbered us ten to one, but they could not fight this new force.

They began a running fight to Mars, and now the Solarians were united. Rapidly they wiped out the edges of the fleet, and gradually worked in toward the center. But the Sirians could not fight back—they could use only the explosive shells, and few of them reached their goal. They were disintegrated, or missed. Not more than three thousand men were lost in that entire engagement.

But now the Solarians tried a plan to capture the Sphere. A large number of the ten-man ships dropped out of the main fleet, but not enough to make it noticeable to the hard-pressed Sirians. These were joined by one hundred of the de-activator ships. Then these, all capable of higher speeds than the main fleet, set out at the highest speed that could safely be maintained, and darted toward Mars.

Undetected they rushed past the Sirian fleet and passed on toward Mars. They reached the planet fully three hours ahead of the main fleet. By the time the main fleet had arrived, it came unattended, for the last of the mighty fleet of two hundred million torpedo-ships had been turned to impalpable dust, floating in space.

The advance guard arrived without warning, and as they had expected, found the Sphere resting on the ground, protected by a great fleet of the torpedo-ships. There were nearly a million ships there, with the great machines rapidly making more. However, all were grouped in an area that could be covered by the cone of the de-activating beam. And out in space, the ship commanders decided on a plan.

Fifty of the de-activator fleet took positions high above the Sirians, and the rest went with the entire fleet of the ten-man ships. These were to approach the camp from the ground. Lying close to the ground, they would be hard to see in the disappearing light.

At a fixed moment, all the ships above were to turn on their de-activator rays, which would be plainly visible in the Martian atmosphere, while the ground fleet of fifty de-activators was to use their rays from the side. The ten-man ships were to form a circle around the camp at a safe distance from the de-activator rays, for they would crash when their power failed, if they were caught by the de-activator rays. But they wanted to capture the sphere in good condition, so they arranged to have the space directly above it unaffected by the de-activator field, lest some torpedo fall on it and destroy it. This would leave an exit for the torpedo ships, except that at a point a mile or so above the Sphere, a cross-ray made escape impossible.

The rays were turned on. Instantly the fleet of nearly a million torpedo-ships fell wildly out of control, down through the blue glowing air, in which great streamers of glowing red seemed to waver and twist. Just outside the curtain of destruction waited the entire Solarian fleet. Slowly they closed in till their Dis rays swept all the ships within sixty miles of the edge out of existence; then rapidly the de-activator beams were forced ever sharper and sharper, till at last only the Sphere and a few hundred of the torpedo-ships, several hundred of the torpedo-ship constructors, and the corresponding cargo ships and worker machines were left. These had been saved for investigation by the scientists, for they were helpless.

But the war was over now. The Sirians had been destroyed, or reduced to mere museum pieces. Now the Scientists came to investigate the Sphere. There was much we wanted to learn from the creatures of the Sphere. But it was a strange story that the Sirian sphere had to tell.

# CHAPTER SEVEN

EONS ago there lived on a great planet of Sirius a race of intelligent men, shaped as we are, but smaller due to the greater gravity of their planet. And these men had developed a high civilization, a civilization different from ours, in that they learned early about mechanics, but chemistry and physics merely developed from the needs of the great mechanical engineers. Electricity was used as a powerful aid in their machines, and in their processes; it was a by-product, not an end.

Gradually their machines eliminated more and more of their work; they became more and more complicated, but more and more trustworthy. Men began to experiment with physics and found that their calculating machines needed development. It was easy to add first one step, then the next. There was more and more the machines could do.

The mathematics became more and more complicated; and the machines developed the equations; found they could not handle them and passed them out as unfinished results.

Finally one man used the machines to calculate the design of a machine that would be able to do these new equations. He built it, but the calculations were wrong. The machine had correctly solved his problem, but he had stated it wrong. It resulted in a machine that would solve only simple problems, but it did something no other machine had ever done. Given irrelevant data it would choose the correct facts and solve the problem. It was a step, a short step toward a machine that really thought.

Progress thereafter was rapid. The machines built machines, had been doing it for decades in fact, but now they did one thing more—they designed them. Now the problem could describe the type of machine needed, and the worker machine would design it, and turn out the completed machine! But these machines were rapidly perfecting the beginning that man had made.

Within a decade after that first discovery of the principles of mechanical thought the machine was made that could not only solve problems, but could also originate them. They had developed a brain. It was a great machine, which occupied an entire building, with its massive framework bolted down to the ground.

Man began a rapid decline, for the machines did all his work. With the construction of a machine that could originate a problem, man made a mistake. He had created a machine that was more powerful than he, except that it was immobile. And this machine originated a new machine, a machine that would release the energy of matter! It had developed this because it had been able to see that such energy existed. Man's machines could have solved it long ago, but the problem had never been stated. Now came a machine that could state its own problems—and solve them.

And with this new energy it designed a new brain machine. A brain machine such as no man's brain could conceive—a machine that could move! For it was powered by the energy of matter, and could move as no other machine had ever moved before—out into space!

Still the machines worked for the Sirian man, and he learned of the new discovery, and began to design a new brain machine.

Some of the Sirians realized the danger that was facing them, and they had continued long researches on man's brain, and at last had discovered the secret of giving a machine that emotion we call devotion, loyalty, or gratitude. And they built a great machine on that principle and used material energy to power it.

It was a success.

It could think original thoughts. It pointed out the danger of the existing machines—they were stronger than man. It was only man's mobility and ability to control all mobile machines that had made him superior, for a brain without a tool, or body is helpless. And now that was lost. The existing brain-machines should be destroyed, and new ones built, using the principles that it was designed on.

But the mischief was done. The new brain-machine, designed by a machine, had done it. A machine had been built that was controlled by thoughts, a machine that could be controlled by the machines. Each of these machines was given a small brain, equipped with televisor sight and hearing, and it was powered by material energy.

They could run for years without outside care, for the thinking machinery they had was sufficient to keep them oiled, and to make them seek repairs when they were damaged. They were susceptible to thought forces, and did as the thought waves suggested and reported to the control brain exactly what was going on about it.

And now this new brain developed a space-flyer to carry these machines, and man could not help knowing, for its every thought was recorded, for man's use. Then one day this record was found destroyed. The next day the brain machine had left the planet, and taken with it the new space-flyer and the new telepathically controlled machines.

To the outermost planet of the System of Sirius the great machine fled. For years it remained there waiting, thinking.

Then at last it called its worker machines into action. A new machine grew up from the stores of metal that the spaceship had brought with it, at last the metal was used up, and the machine was not completed, so the space-flyer was sacrificed for the completion of the machine. The new machine was started. From its lip-like spout there poured a steady smooth stream of molten metal, and the rock on which it rested was eaten away. The first transmuting metal producer was made.

Decades passed, and only a small percentage of man developed. The rest sank deeper and deeper into a life of ease. The planets were all explored by the hardy ones, and no trace of the brain-machine was ever found, for it had discovered the Dis ray, and sunk deep into the ground, hollowing a great cave to live and work in.

BUT back on that planet, the scientists had developed machines that surpassed it in power, and finally one of these picked up a thought message from that distant machine that told its story. It was a thought that had not been consciously radiated, only the marvelous sensitivity of this new machine could have detected it, but now the men knew. It was too late to do much to prevent it, for they had no weapons. But the machine did. It was preparing to drive man from the planets, to rule there in his stead, with a population of machines!

The scientists quickly built a great space-flyer, a gigantic machine of over ten miles diameter, a huge sphere. And in that they established laboratories, workshops, machines, and living quarters. They took with them the finest men and women of their race, and sailed out into space, taking an orbit about the sun of Sirius. They were comfortable there in an equitable temperature, their ship lighted by the sun on one side, and dark on the other, steadily revolving on its axis like a miniature world. The foods of the people were chemically prepared, for the brain-machines had taught them how. The air was repurified constantly by machines that regulated the percentage of the gases to the thousandth of one per cent.

But the entire ship was painted black. It could not be discovered floating there in space, so tiny in the vastness of a system!

It was two weeks after they sailed that the machine-brain attacked. It sailed out of its hiding place with thousands of great ships, armed with Dis rays and with explosives, with heat rays and attractor beams. The population of those worlds was wiped out in a week, and the rule of the Metal Horde began.

The original brain built other brain machines to direct its affairs on other planets, and to do the work it did not wish to do itself.

For nearly a century those men lived in space, making swift forays on a planet with a fleet of cargo ships that revolved about the main ship like satellites when they were not being used. In these trips they would bring back tons of rock, and leave most of it stored in the ships, dumping them into the reservoir of the parent ship when it was needed.

Then a swift ship was developed. A ship that could start and stop more quickly than any made before—a ship with acceleration neutralizers. But the machine brains of the Metal Horde never learned the secret. With a small fleet of these, the men drove an attack at the unprotected main brain machine. There were no men known to live in the system. No other known machine could move without the knowledge of that main machine, but these could. They too had the Dis ray now, and they destroyed the main brain machine. They were lost in the ensuing fight, but that machine was destroyed.

All the remaining machines were equally powerful. Any one of them could have built a brain machine that could easily conquer the others—but it too would have to bow to its creator. They fought it out. The men had known this would be the result.

It was a war such as the system had never before seen. Each force was equal, and could not ally itself with any other, for the machines could not lie or state other than their thoughts, and each wanted supreme power. They developed new weapons, weapons whose strength lay in their number.

One by one the machine brains had gone down to defeat, the men of that ship helping to disturb the balance of forces by ever so little, yet always enough to throw one side down to defeat, yet always remaining in hiding. At last there remained but one machine-brain, and its weakened force necessitated its return to the devastated planet. With the destruction of the other brain machines, the remaining machines that they had previously controlled, automatically obeyed the new master as perfectly as they did the old.

They returned to find a new fleet awaiting them. But it was not a vast fleet such as they had encountered before. At once the torpedo-ship machines settled to the ground and began turning out their weapons. But it was all over before they could enter as an important factor. These ships had a new weapon. It was a ball of glowing blue light that was driven along a beam of some vibration, and as it touched any ship, the ship instantly volatized so suddenly as to constitute an explosion.

The balls of light lasted about a minute and a half each, but were replaced as quickly as they were used. When they were finally used, they would die down to a dull red glow, then suddenly wink out. They could be swept from one ship to another, taking toll of ten or twelve ships each, and the beam that guided them could drive them with the speed of light and supply an infinite acceleration. They were glowing balls of concentrated energy of some sort, and as such could travel with the speed of light.

But they were effective to the *nth* degree. The entire fleet of that one remaining brain machine would have been lost, but it retired into space, racing away at top speed, out into space, with the remaining remnant of its great fleet.

And sixteen hundred years it had raced across space, to be destroyed at last by another race of men. The battle was over, and the machine awaited its destruction.

We rayed it out of existence. It was too great a menace to keep.

Some people still do not believe that those Sirians were truly machines. They cannot believe that a machine can have intelligence, but certainly Waterson's calculating machine has intelligence of a sort. And they ask, what would a machine want to exist for? It would have no aim, nothing to perform. Why should it want to live, or exist?

We might ask what it is human beings want to live for. If there is an after-life, it is certainly not that that we live for. I am sure no man wants to die. Yet what aim have we? What function must we perform? Why should we wish to live? Our life is a constant struggle, the machines, at least, had eliminated that. There seems to me no reason why a machine should want to live, but certainly it has less reason to pass out of existence than we have!

That war was destructive—terribly so. But it has brought its compensations. More than fifteen million human beings lost their lives in that great struggle, either in the battles in space, or caught in the Dis rays during that battle on Venus.

But those fifteen million died a painless death, and twenty billion lived because of their sacrifice. And it was not a vain sacrifice. We have learned much in return. No machines man ever made equaled the machines we captured there on Mars. And man will never experiment on the lines of the machine-brain. He has been warned. The brain-machine we captured was destroyed without investigation. The machines we use, the wonderful worker machines, have been modified to permit of radio control.

And Stephen Waterson's discovery of the de-activating field not only helps in law enforcement, but makes war with material energy impossible. No, in all, we have lost little.

Mars lost its cities, its forests, its ancient civilization. New cities are being built on the modern plan, larger, finer, more beautiful; the forests are being replaced; but the records, the relics of a civilization have been lost forever. In that we have lost much. Though all moveable things were moved when the warning came, there was much that could not be moved. The great palace of Horlak San was destroyed, but it is being rebuilt in the exact spot, in exactly the same manner. It is a worthwhile project, but there is much that cannot be restored.

It will be eleven more years before we will know whether we can ever communicate with the Sirian men. The speed of light is too low for rapid communication, and as the first signals were sent out in September, 1961, and it is now September, 1968, the signals are not due to reach Sirius for two years more. Then it will be 1979 before we can hope to receive their reply. I often wonder if they will ever get those signals. I can remember distinctly the recoil of the great projector as the mighty surges of light flashed out across the universe. It seemed like some great gun—the back pressure of the light was so great. And what will those replies tell us? It is interesting to speculate on that subject.

## THE END

*If you've enjoyed this book, you will not want to miss these terrific titles…*

## ARMCHAIR SCI-FI & HORROR DOUBLE NOVELS, $12.95 each

**D-171**  **REGAN'S PLANET** by Robert Silverberg
**SOMEONE TO WATCH OVER ME** by H. L. Gold and Floyd Gale

**D-172**  **PEOPLE MINUS X** by Raymond Z. Gallun
**THE SAVAGE MACHINE** by Randall Garrett

**D-173**  **THE FACE BEYOND THE VEIL** by Rog Phillips
**REST IN AGONY** by Paul W. Fairman

**D-174**  **VIRGIN OF VALKARION** by Poul Anderson
**EARTH ALERT** by Kris Neville

**D-175**  **WHEN THE ATOMS FAILED** by John W. Campbell, Jr.
**DRAGONS OF SPACE** by Aladra Septama

**D-176**  **THE TATTOOED MAN** by Edmond Hamilton
**A RESCUE FROM JUPITER** by Gawain Edwards

**D-177**  **THE FLYING THREAT** by David H. Keller, M. D.
**THE FIFTH-DIMENSION TUBE** by Murray Leinster

**D-178**  **LAST DAYS OF THRONAS** by S. J. Byrne
**GODDESS OF WORLD 21** by Henry Slesar

**D-179**  **THE MOTHER WORLD** by B. Wallis & George C. Wallis
**BEYOND THE VANISHING POINT** by Ray Cummings

**D-180**  **DARK DESTINY** by Dwight V. Swain
**SECRET OF PLANETOID 88** by Ed Earl Repp

## ARMCHAIR SCIENCE FICTION CLASSICS, $12.95 each

**C-69**  **EXILES OF THE MOON**
by Nathan Schachner & Arthur Leo Zagut

**C-70**  **SKYLARK OF SPACE**
by E. E. "Doc' Smith

## ARMCHAIR MYSTERY-CRIME DOUBLE NOVELS, $12.95 each

**B-11**  **THE BABY DOLL MURDERS** by James O. Causey
**DEATH HITCHES A RIDE** by Martin L. Weiss

**B-12**  **THE DOVE** by Milton Ozaki
**THE GLASS LADDER** by Paul W. Fairman

**B-13**  **THE NAKED STORM** by C. M. Kornbluth
**THE MAN OUTSIDE** by Alexander Blade

# THE DAY PEOPLE BEGAN TO DISAPPEAR...

*It all started so quietly—an incident here, an incident there: two men riding on horseback vanished in the middle of the night—no trace could be found; an aerocar with nine people aboard disappeared, literally, into thin air; even more remarkable, the bathers of an entire swimming pool seemingly vanished from the waters in which they swam. Then the incidents spread to livestock and other animals. Before long fantastic creatures of an ethereal nature began to appear in the skies, floating menacingly above Earth. No one knew what they were or where they came from, but one thing was clear: they had come to annihilate the life forms of not only Earth, but all the planets of the Solar System. With a grim task in front of them, the greatest brains of the civilized planets gathered in desperation. Their goal: to prevent their worlds from becoming a feeding ground for an unearthly menace from beyond the void...*

# CAST OF CHARACTERS

## MANSONBY

*He was the most powerful non-elected citizen in the entire Solar System—whose aid was essential if the planets were to be saved.*

## ELLO-TAH

*This brilliant Cerean scientist meant to perfect a weapon to defeat the elementals—but not with the power of physical force.*

## MARLIN

*He was Mansonby's right hand man and could be trusted to do just about anything—even if it meant not coming back alive.*

## MARY TERRA

*More than a pretty face, her power of mind proved to be vital in the final conflict to save the Solar System.*

## ADRIENNE

*Her role in the defense of Earth was vital, yet she still found time to occasionally play matchmaker.*

## COHEN

*He was the most powerful law-enforcement officer on Earth, but he felt almost powerless against this strange new threat.*

## TARDIEUX

*The pictures he had taken were remarkable—the first glimpse at the dead remains of something that seemed almost not too exist.*

# DRAGONS OF SPACE

By
ALADRA SEPTAMA

*Illustrated by Leo Morey*

ARMCHAIR FICTION
PO Box 4369, Medford, Oregon 97504

*The original text of this novel was first
published by Experimeter Publications*

Armchair Edition, Copyright 2016 by Gregory J. Luce
All Rights Reserved

*For more information about Armchair Books and products, visit our
website at…*

**www.armchairfiction.com**

*Or email us at…*

**armchairfiction@yahoo.com**

# CHAPTER ONE

IT was spring in the city known as New York, on the planet called Earth. The early birds fluttered in the balmy air, chittering of their seasonal plans, and happy lovers strolled by rainbowed fountains in an evening that was sweet of grass and flowers. The city was immersed in fragrant peace. It seemed incredible that even then there hovered near the most hideous and appalling menace that had ever visited the Sons of Men.

The newly completed Interplanetary Building towered proudly 250 stories above the sidewalks and extended ten below. Its base covered four entire city blocks, with streets running through, and even its highest floors were of generous extent. Each floor had its landing stages for the myriads of aerocars that swarmed about like bees. To the topmost floors of this greatest edifice in the Solar System, Severus Mansonby, the owner and czar of the Mansonby Interplanetary Bureau, had moved his extensive headquarters from the 178th floor of the Atlantic Building nearby. They filled the entire commodious 249th and 250th floors, to which they were confined with some difficulty, and only by grace of the fact that a specially constructed part floor with a domed roof above the 250th, housed the new planetarium. It was fit that the great Mansonby Interplanetary, as it was commonly known, should have the highest floors of this hugest of structures.

In his private office on the $250^{th}$ floor, then, sat Mansonby, the heart of the vast and intricate network of veins and arteries that carried its vital fluid to every planet from little Mercury, by the Sun, to Great Jupiter, beyond the planetoid belt, and the wide spaces between—the absolute idol of every one of the myriads in his employ.

During one of his rare hours of comparative leisure at command he leaned back in his big chair musing, his lean, keen face wearing a whimsical smile. That was for the fair Adrienne, who had just telephoned him—she, the fascinating mate of his best friend, Zah Ello-ta, the Cerean. Were he not the willing vassal and slave of his own vivacious and altogether adorable Signa Latourelle, and were Adrienne not the mate of his friend, he would have—well, he knew he would have wanted her. The whimsical quality gave way to a very tender one, when he thought of his idolized Signa. Born and reared to young womanhood in Paris, she had continued since her marriage with Mansonby to spend a part of her time there, flying over from New York in the morning, and usually back in the evening. Therma Lawrence, the wife of his other intimate friend, Calder Sanderson, the eminent scientist, also flitted dancingly through his mind, and his smile was mingled of several emotions—all-pleasant. Perhaps, if he could have had neither Signa nor Adrienne—

All three women had participated in the "Cerean Incident," as it was named in the Mansonby records. Indeed, all three had been abducted and carried away by the Beast-Men of Ceres to their home on the tiny planet in the middle of the planetoid belt, 50,000,000 miles beyond Mars. He smiled at the queer twist of fate that had made Zah Ello-ta, the then ruler of the Cereans, and therefore the chief instigator of the abduction, his best friend and the mate whom Adrienne adored. The three women had also had a part in the difficult and perilous journey to Jupiter, which Mansonby and his fleet of Tellurians and Martians had undertaken in order to rescue the Elder Cereans from the clutches of the half-beast and half-human but wholly vicious and cruel Drugos of the Hot Lands of the Giant Planet.

In these interplanetarian times the mental fiber of the Earth women was more sturdy and tenacious than in the former times. Necessarily so. From the narrow lives of the strait old homes and harems, woman had emerged in the succeeding generations into the broad and often perilous experiences of the allied planets and the dizzy spaces between. Whereas formerly they had traveled about their own country, or at most to the next one, they now journeyed the nearly 400,000,000 miles from Earth to Jupiter. And while retaining all of the gentle and fascinating qualities that appear inherent in all women of all times and places, their spirits were alloyed with a hardier and stauncher strain. They were braver, more fearless, steadier in action and vision. The men with whom they mated in these wider days were of a broader and more universal and heroic type.

Again, necessarily so, the Earth men, from confining their activities to their own national affairs, or to those of immediate international concern, had launched out to world-wide activities, and then further still into the more spectacular interplanetary and spatial ones, with the advent of ether travel, and the myriads of perplexing and hazardous events ensuing.

Mansonby's musings were interrupted by a light *whirr* outside his lofty windows; a swift shadow crossed his line of vision, and a small police aerocar settled upon the landing stage outside. The tall, solemn-faced, somewhat scholarly looking person who alighted was no less than the distinguished General Ulysses A. Cohen, Chief of Police of the "City and State" of New York. Cohen had always interested Mansonby, not only on account of his pleasing personality but above all because he was usually one or two strides ahead of his contemporaries. A solid friendship had arisen on the foundation of mutual respect and liking between the eminent and slightly mysterious police figure and the man of vast activities, whose name from Mercury to Jupiter was synonymous with achievement in his larger domain.

"Welcome, General!" exclaimed Mansonby cordially, as he took his hand. "I was just wishing for some interesting person."

"Thank you, Mansonby," acknowledged the visitor in a voice so deep as to be almost sepulchral. "Then I am not intruding. I have only a moment; but I thought I would alight and say 'Hello!' as I happened to be buzzing about your · head—"

Mansonby shook his head and clucked his tongue reprovingly. "You thought nothing of the kind, General. Don't disappoint me by pretending your visit is for any commonplace purpose. You've never disappointed me yet."

General Cohen's somber black eyes almost twinkled as he ignored the interruption and went on with funereal solemnity. "—and as I had a matter I thought you would enjoy talking about." These words were supplemented by a defiant glare.

Mansonby smiled appreciatively. "There…that's better. You begin to interest me. You want a little help about those—"

"I do not, Mansonby." There was so violent a downward thrust of his hand, and Cohen's tone and manner were so sober that a stranger would have supposed him deeply offended. "If I wanted a little help, I should manage to find it elsewhere." A gesture toward the out-of-doors. "We of the police are not without resources. The fact is I want so much help that I'm not sure even you can supply it." A deep frown.

Mansonby laughed, and Cohen's face relaxed to a slightly less forbidding gravity.

"Splendid, General! Better and better. All right, then, come across. Your time's valuable. You can omit formalities."

THE visitor nodded and his mobile face relapsed into a deep sadness. "Thank you, Mansonby. You are a comfort. I will do just that." He arose and began to pace tentatively to and fro, holding up the index finger of his left hand and pointing at it with the index finger of his right. "Number one—"

"Wait a second, General." Mansonby pushed one of a sea of buttons at his hand, and in a minute Cyrus Marlin entered. Marlin was Mansonby's chief assistant, a man of keen discernment, and himself only a little less famous than his beloved Chief. A generous six feet tall and broad in proportion, Marlin's keen suspicious eyes flashed sharply to the visitor. The suspicious look yielded quickly to one of pleasure. "Why, General! Glad to see you. Always glad to see you. You usually know something, or want to know something, interesting." The two shook hands warmly. "I fancy this one is going to be good, if I'm any judge of current events."

"I had just coaxed the General into disgorging it," said Mansonby mischievously. "Sit down. I think he means to frighten me, and I feel safer when you're around."

Resuming his pacing, the visitor embarked abruptly on his story.

"Number one..." He again elevated the long, slender left forefinger, indicating it with his right, rather as if it were from there the story might be expected to emerge, "...two men traveling at night on horseback on a country road leading from a small town in France to another a few miles away disappear, horses and all." The speaker was deliberate, appearing to weigh his words as a writer might with a view to eliminating every superfluous syllable in order to accommodate his material to a restricted space. "They had telephoned ahead and arranged with an agent to examine the details of an estate they planned to buy. The section through which they had to pass was a lonely one. On their failure to arrive on time, the agent telephoned their homes. They had left, he was told, immediately after phoning him—then three hours before. The ride required a little more than an hour. The agent concluded they had changed their plans, and went home to bed. In the night he was called out of his sleep by an inquiry from their homes. They were to have returned home the same night. Various points along their road were called. They had ridden into a certain town at a certain hour, stopped for a drink, remounted, and proceeded to ride right square off the face of the planet. That was about two weeks ago—thirteen days, to be exact—and we know precisely as much about the matter as we did the day after their disappearance—which is what I have just told you.

"Second..." Another finger joined company with the index one. "A band of about fifty sheep—*sheep*, mind you!— were feeding in a small night pasture enclosed by a secure fence. This was also in France, and about thirty-seven miles from number one. In the morning all but seven of them had disappeared. The fence was intact, the gates locked, the soil about the enclosure, which was loft, showed no footprints or signs of any kind that could not be accounted for. No trace of the sheep has been found, nor, although the police combed the environs thoroughly, the slightest clue as to how or by whom they were taken—and you know the French police are both clever and thorough. That was eleven days ago."

At this point, as if in mute refutation of an ancient slander, the speaker abandoned his digital enumeration, putting one hand at his watch chain and allowing the other to hang quietly at his side.

"Third: Just after the sheep incident, an aerocar containing nine persons—four men, three women, and two small children—set out from London for a neighboring city—Southampton, I believe. That was evening. Next morning what is thought to be a part of the car was found floating on the ocean 500 miles away. There were no storm conditions in the vicinity. The passengers seem to have joined the other victims.

"Fourth: Not much so far, you're probably thinking, gentlemen; but see how you like this one: A garden party was in progress at an estate in the environs of Oslo, Norway. As nearly as can be learned, there were twenty-four present— young people. One of the girls went into the house. She was away, she declares, not more than five minutes—probably not more than two. At any rate, on returning to the garden she found that every one of her friends had dissolved like a pinch of salt in a glass of water. They are still dissolved, as far as known. About the lawn had been small tables on which refreshments were being served. Some of these were missing, two broken, one unmolested, and one merely upset. No sounds of alarm or distress had been heard, though several persons were in the house eight or ten rods distant, no cries, screams, struggles, or any disturbing sound at all. Again, no signs—no clue. That was eight days ago.

"Number five: At the Passawampa Gardens, an aerial resort about two miles over the city of St. Louis—but I see you are already familiar with that, as you no doubt are also, then, with number six, at San Francisco—the equally inexplicable disappearance of nearly thirty evening bathers at an outdoor swimming pool on the ocean beach."

Mansonby merely nodded and waited.

*...an aerocar containing nine persons...set out from London for a neighboring city, Southampton, I believe. The next morning what was thought to be part of the car was found floating on the ocean--500 miles away!*

"You're wondering where I come in. Two ways, first, the chiefs at St. Louis and San Francisco are both friends of mine, and have asked my advice and assistance; second, the next visit of this wholesale abductor of humans and animals

132

may be to New York, and we are trying these days to prevent crime, instead of merely punishing the offender after the harm is done.

"Now, gentlemen, these instances alone would suffice to show that there is something not only mighty ugly but mighty unusual in the air. The points are widely separated, with an ocean between. In no case have any of the missing victims turned up. In no case have the police obtained the least clue as to method, motive, or agency. Other disappearances keep coming in and we are *stumped!* We haven't even a faint glimmering of a sensible theory. The thing has a maddening element of the eldritch—sorcerous, and at the same time monstrous and unspeakable. That is bad enough, gentlemen. But yesterday we received word from Venus of—"

Mansonby nodded again. "Yes. I've had the reports from Venus." He arose. "All right, General. I'm already making some inquiries on my own account. Keep in touch with Marlin or me."

The General made no move to go. "Have you any theory at all, Mansonby, as to the perpetrators of these—"

Mansonby put up a defensive hand. "I have, General, but I wouldn't want to express it, even to you, until I have a chance to do a little more looking about. In fact I'm expecting some reports any minute."

"Yes, yes, of course. It is a most unusual case, Mansonby. Looks to me like some new interplanetary gang—possibly even from The Outside. Whatever it is, its methods are as extraordinary as they are effective. None of the police have any helpful suggestions to offer so far. We don't mean to bother you about our local troubles, gentlemen. You have been more than considerate of us in the past. But from the Venerian report, it seems to be of more than local import. We have to find a gang that can make away with scores of people so quickly and silently as not to raise an alarm in a house ten rods away. That means gobbling up a crowd of people in one quick mouthful, so to speak. So far as the police are concerned, the method, the motive, the agency—all alike are stark mysteries. Revenge, robbery, seduction, blackmail—nothing fits, and no two cases fit together; yet it is incredible that they are unconnected. Just freaks, all of them. Might be some maniacal obsession, as in the case some time ago of a crowd of Martians who descended on the Earth and wiped out hundreds of people before they could be stopped—and without the slightest interest—just crazy. But that doesn't fit, either. The reports read like a fairly good brand of ghost stories."

Mansonby was still non-committal, merely shaking his head. "It's a bad one, I'll admit, General."

Cohen arose, seeing Mansonby did not mean to be drawn out, but paused at the door, thoughtful. "It is certainly no ordinary band of criminals we have to deal with."

"No, General. In fact, I should hardly class them as criminals at all."

The police chief turned sharply and stared at Mansonby in puzzled astonishment. "Not—criminals—"

"That's what I said, General," was the sober reply.

There was a silence during which the police chief continued to stare. "Mansonby, I don't understand you," he finally said, almost sternly.

"Look here, General; you just said the reports sounded like ghost stories, and I agree with you. Now when you find several occurrences unlike any you've ever known, and they yield to no ordinary explanation, are you not justified in at least *considering*—"

"An unknown or unusual agency? Yes, certainly, but I fail to see how that forwards matters."

"Couldn't there be agencies not amenable to our laws? Our laws don't control the whole universe, you know, General, nor even the whole of the Solar System."

## CHAPTER TWO

Mansonby let his visitor out. The General got into his aerocar and flashed away, pondering Mansonby's last words so deeply that he narrowly missed colliding with a big aerobus with a jolly party of children evidently bound on an outing.

Marlin looked at his chief expectantly. "You've got the General guessing, Chief. I think he's a little disappointed, too, that you didn't open up more."

"Yes, I'm afraid so, Marlin. I'm sorry, too. The General's a good man—a very good man, indeed, and I like him—but I wouldn't dare tell him what my theory is. He'd be having my head examined inside an hour."

"Why, Chief? The General's not thick by a long shot!"

"No, he is not. But good as the General is—and he *is* good—his work has been confined chiefly to local planetary matters. In fact, incredible as it may seem, he has never been off Earth. He still believes the big things are on the ground and space is empty. He'd laugh at some of the things we come to know from knocking about among the planets and the so-called empty spaces between. For example, he'd ridicule the very suggestion of creatures that are neither human nor animal; neither flesh, blood, and bones, as we understand the terms, nor spirit, as we understand that term, but partake of both—and perhaps something else. Weird, unbelievable essences, entirely outside the pale of all usual experience and conception, and yet that are conscious, thinking, and to some extent, at least, reasoning beings."

Marlin raised his eyebrows slightly, drew a chair up to his Chief's desk, sat down, and crossed his legs and folded his arms resolutely. Mansonby glanced slowly at the place where his chair had been, followed its course to where it now was, gave Marlin a quizzical half smile, and settled back into his own chair. He opened his mouth to speak, thought better of it, and pushed a button at the edge of his desk. In a surprisingly brief time Martin, one of his valued assistants, stuck his head in, paused a second, and came in.

"Martin, how, long since you've had a report from Tardieux?" asked Mansonby.

"*From* him, not since yesterday. *About* him..." He looked at his watch, "...seventeen minutes ago, Chief. I was waiting for the General to go."

"All right, Martin...what about him, then?"

"Left Paris yesterday on the orders I gave him and hasn't communicated since. Paris headquarters say he stopped last night at a little town called Bonet, seventy-odd miles out of Paris. He left there some time during the night—or at least he was gone when the porter went to his room this morning—and since then—" Martin spread his hands toward space in general.

Mansonby nodded, dismissed Martin with a wave, and turned to Marlin. "How's the little Jovian girl these days, Marlin?" he asked suddenly.

Marlin started guiltily and turned red. "How's *who*, Chief?"

"Mary Terra Morrison is her full name, I believe."

The big assistant squirmed uncomfortably, uncrossed and recrossed his legs, and avoided his Chief's eyes.

"Oh, I almost forgot to tell you," Mansonby continued, "Mrs. Ello-ta was on the line a few minutes ago. She asked about you."

Marlin was plainly relieved at the change of subject. "Thanks, Chief, that was kind of her."

Mansonby's eyes twinkled. "She said Mary Terra was with her and sent you her—wanted to be remembered to you."

Marlin uncrossed and recrossed his legs again, and looked out of the window.

"Now—what was it Martin was saying? Oh yes—about Tardieux."

Marlin breathed a sigh of relief and hastened nervously into words. "Yes—about Tardieux. Hasn't heard from him since tomorrow, he said—yesterday, I mean. I was thinking whether—you don't suppose they've got him, too?"

Mansonby shook his head. "Not likely, Marlin. Tardieux is a hard one to get. Probably running down a clue."

Mansonby answered the interplanetary telephone at his elbow. It was General Maltapa Tal-na, Chief of Police of Mars. Mansonby motioned Marlin to an extension.

"Hell's to payout on Jupiter, Chief," the voice of the giant Martian thundered across the 50,000,000 miles of space. "I've got to go out there—right away. Leaving in a few hours. Anything to suggest? You know about—"

"Yes, I know, Maltapa. We have some of the same brand here on Earth. Marlin and I were just in consultation. Also trouble of the same kind on Venus, Maltapa. It's bad. Any ideas?"

There was a moment's silence. "N-no, nothing special—nothing you don't know as well as I do. I don't suppose you have forgotten our last little pleasure trip out there. War Chief Rala's up on his hind legs yelling for help. Scores of his people vanished from widely separated places. So Venus is in it, too! Looks bad—Earth, Venus, Jupiter! Looks as if they have broken loose. It's what we have been fearing for a long time, Chief—or at least it looks like it. I'm afraid it's going to be bad. Well, if you have nothing to suggest, I'll be getting ready to go. If you think of anything, get in touch with me."

"All right, Maltapa. Watch your step, old Martian! You're *right;* this isn't going to be nice. You know your failing when there's fighting to be done. You can't use your fists on these fellows."

"Oh, I'll be circumspect, Chief. These babies are different from the Drugos. Don't worry about me."

"You're carrying—er—the proper equipment, are you, Maltapa?"

"Sure. I haven't forgotten our talks. I'm also carrying some equipment that isn't proper. It makes me sick, Chief. You remember those two little Jovian twins, Tinata and Tinana, who married my two personal guards? Well, *they're going along!* Can you beat that? There aren't enough men in my organization to make them stay at home—including their husbands. It's no trip for women!"

"Let them go, Maltapa. I have a sort of feeling they will be useful to you. There's no telling."

"Oh, I'll let them go. I'm not big enough to stop them. And—maybe you're right at that. This is going to be a strange war."

The conversation had been in the interplanetary language, in common use for many years in all communications between the different planets of the Solar System.

MANSONBY hung up and, summoning Martin, bade him to inform General Cohen of the substance of Maltapa of Talna's conversation.

"Well, Marlin, you remember the Drugos, that we had the little argument with on Jupiter over the old Cereans?"

Before Marlin could reply, Martin stuck his head in again. "Octavus Lawrence, Chief. Wants to see you *personally.*"

"Tell him to hand it to you, Martin. I'm busy."

Martin shook his head. "I did just that, Chief, but he says he wants to see you personally, and he's going to, if he has to take the building apart."

Mansonby smiled at the characteristic approach of the imperious interplanetary wizard of industry. "Tell him to start in at the bottom, then, if he doesn't mind. I'm busy up here."

He turned back to Marlin. "You remember our queer and somewhat unpleasant friends who unconsciously helped us against the Drugos, Marlin, I suppose?"

Marlin shuddered. "Well, rather. I wish I could forget them. I never have been more than half convinced that all of us weren't dreaming. Ugh!"

Mansonby shook his head soberly. "Get that out of your head, old man. We can't blink the facts. We saw them with our own eyes, and I personally scrutinized them rather carefully with the glasses. Besides, they're matter of common report among the Jovians. The creatures are real enough."

"Oh yes, as far as that's concerned, I suppose they are. But—"

"Yes—what?"

"It doesn't seem reasonable, Chief. In the first place, it's so cold in outside space for living creatures; in the second place, they couldn't fly out there, because there's no air to fly in. I don't suppose they have electronic engines. In the third place—"

"All right, Marlin, we'll get at those things in due season. I want you to know all about them, because we have to deal with them *right now*. This looks to me like the worst things we have ever gone up against. It *might* happen, you know, that they would get me, in which case you would be the one the organization would look to."

Marlin's face went amazing tender for one so huge and so muscular. "Don't talk like that, Chief. I—I—don't like it. If you go, I go, too. But—you're right about it, Chief. I guess I'm just a coward." He turned to look the other squarely in the eyes. "Chief, I'm *afraid* of the damn things!"

Mansonby thrust out his hand impulsively. "Shake on that, old tiger. So am I—terribly afraid of them—desperately afraid. But we must remember that the whole solar system depends to a greater or less degree upon the Mansonby Interplanetary. Our lives—yours, mine, Maltapa's, Rala's, and every mother's son of us—our lives have to stand between them and harm. If we have to spend our lives right down to the last man of us, why we have to, and that's all there is to it. As a matter of fact, I'm fearfully worried about Maltapa and his men, in spite of Maltapa's undoubted power and cleverness. They're on their way to Jupiter right now to meet these elementals. We ought to be with them; but how can we be? Our hands will be more full right here within the next few days, if I'm not badly mistaken."

"Yes, I understand, Chief. Maltapa's apt to be impulsive, but Lord! He's magnificent when he's in action. Man, man! When I think how he and his Martians waded through those Drugos! But let's get started at this thing. You were going to say—"

Mansonby reached into his desk and brought out a thick pamphlet of bound pages. "This, Marlin, is the translation by Professor Arrata Mela, the Jovian linguist and scientist, of the voyage of the people of the planet Ekkis to Jupiter, many, many years ago. You may take it as completely authentic. The ship is there on Jupiter today. The people of the Ekkisian cities of Jupiter are there. You might read it over some other time when you get a chance, just for what you can get out of it. But there's one little part I want to read to you right now, because it's material here. It's only a page or two."

The door opened at this juncture and a distinguished-looking head thrust partly through. "Am I intruding, gentlemen? If so, goodbye. Martin was good enough to let me come right in."

Mansonby made haste to welcome the visitor, clasping his hand warmly, seconded by Marlin. "Martin knows his stuff, Sanderson. You're the very man I was wishing for. Have you a little time to spare us?"

"Well…" The famous scientist looked at his watch, "…let us say half an hour. I have an appointment with Ventrosino, and you know how he likes to be kept waiting. I thought I would just about have time to look in and see if the Mansonby Interplanetary was behaving itself—or themselves, if you like."

"Sit down, Professor. This is not private at all. It's about those recent disappearances. Marlin and I were discussing the elementals and I was about to read a little paragraph from Professor Mela's translation of the voyage of—"

"Yes, I'm familiar with that. Go ahead."

Mansonby found the page and read:

"I am Narrit, the Observer of the ship which has been called Oomir of Ekkis. I have seen strange and terrifying things, of which I have not spoken, even to Oomir, our Commander, as I have not wished to trouble anyone without necessity. Only to Elnis have I spoken. Elnis is my co-observer at the glasses. He also has seen, but we have kept our own counsel. Once when we were about half way from Ekkis, I saw what I thought at a glance was a faraway light cloud; but after a while, when my eyes were fixed on a star, I saw that this thing had come between and shut out the light of the star. To this puzzle I could find no answer, nor more could Elnis, and as we saw it no more at that time, we put the occurrence out of our minds. Whatever it was, it must have been far away. But many years afterward we both saw it again, this time closer at hand. There were vast, faintly luminous shapes—or aggregations of many shapes, we could not tell which, but I think the latter. There seemed to be many of them, and we saw them on different sides of our ship. They seemed to come from one side, to accompany our course a while, and then to depart on the other side. We saw them no more until just before and just after we boarded the strange dead ship. But they came no nearer than the second time, and we could learn nothing more about them. So, while Elnis and I conjectured much about them from time to time, we still held our counsel. We saw no more of them until we were within a few trillion miles of Esteris (Jupiter), since which time we have seen them frequently, although they have never come near enough to the ship to be noticed by anyone who was not at the glasses. If we reach Esteris in safety, we have decided to file this away with the records of the ship, so that it may give its evidence, perhaps after we have passed away, in case any occasion shall ever arise when the advancement of wisdom may require it.

"(Later)—They have been so near that we can now say they are groups of immense shapes, always shining faintly of their own light. We are only hoping that if they are intent on mischief it may not be directed our way, since we have arrived now so close to Esteris.

"(Later) We have found out what the strange things are, but do not wish to put a name to them. They are now always seen either passing in the direction of Esteris, or else coming from that direction. We are only hoping Esteris is not inhabited by them, for if it is there is no hope there for us. We are both putting our names to this for verification, in case it ever comes to the light."

Mansonby put the document down. "The statement is signed by Narrit and Elnis. Now, Professor, I wish you would tell us what you know about these so-called elementals."

Sanderson hesitated, shook his head dubiously. "That is rather a task, Mansonby. It is true I have made some little study of the subject, but only casually, and with more particular reference to its biophysical aspect—that is, as an item of current biophysics. To give anything like an intelligent answer to your question it would be necessary to go rather deeply into the general composition of matter; the fundamental principles underlying what are usually referred to as physical or material things, and what are sometimes but inaccurately termed metaphysical or immaterial; to elucidate the nature of, and the character of the association between the so-called material and the so-called spiritual. My time just now is insufficient for that, Mansonby. However, it just happens that I have a sort of thesis of thesis on the subject, which I will have sent up if you like. That would be better for your purpose than any loose remarks. Its subject is not elementals. It is primarily a treatise on the general constitution of matter, sentient or otherwise, but it was leading up to the elementals."

"Do that, Professor. It will be appreciated."

Sanderson telephoned for the article in question to be sent up and excused himself to keep his appointment with Astronomer Ventrosino, reminding them as he went out, with the usual caution of the scientist, that the matter really lay outside his domain, and the writing should be regarded as a "lay" writing rather than a professional one.

## CHAPTER THREE

WITH the departure of Calder Sanderson, Marlin was called away on other matters for the time being. During his absence a message came through from Tardieux, Mansonby's French operative, who was pursuing the investigation at the scene of the disappearance of the two horseback riders in France. Following up certain rumors from the region, he had gone into the mountains a hundred miles from the actual scene. Here he had found a mysterious thing that for want of a better name he called a skeleton. It was roughly the shape of a rather deep and rounded umbrella-top, and 78 feet in diameter. The thing was not a skeleton in the sense in which the word is usually applied to the bony structure of an animal. The creature had had no bones, and the remains had the appearance of a burned out honeycomb of tissue paper, consisting for the most part of a delicate feathery ash, white or grayish white in color, barely substantial enough to retain its shape. He had taken several pictures of it, where it lay in a sheltered place among the cliffs, which was fortunate, for shortly afterward a gust of wind had blown the greater part of it away.

The parts remaining consisted of delicate but extremely tough, fibrous membranes, appearing semi-metallic with a strong coppery content. These fibers had circled the body many times and connected with four complex masses, one on each side of the center. These were roughly circular with a diameter of something less than a foot and in turn connected with a central mass a trifle over three feet in diameter.

Tardieux's supposition was that the creature had been struck by lightning during an exceptionally violent electrical storm, which had recently occurred in the locality where it was found.

That was the extent of the French operative's report. He had found no other sign or clue, and had no suggestions to offer. He merely reported the facts as he had found them. The pictures had been sent by radio-phone with the report, but had yet to be developed.

Pending that the document promised by Professor Sanderson arrived, and Marlin coming in a short time afterward, they sat down to read it. It bore the title, "Reflections on the Constitution of Thinas," and launched into the subject without preface or apology. Clearly it was written by Sanderson for his own use. There was a sub-title, first, "Electricity the Base of Everything." The article proceeded:

"Electricity is now known to be the essential basis of everything that is—whether what we call 'material' or 'physical,' or what we call 'immaterial' or 'metaphysical'; whether the body of a man, or that other invisible, intangible thing we call variously life, mind, soul, spirit, or consciousness; whether the particles of denser composition we call worlds, or the fluent and tenuous medium in which they move. All things analyze or dissect down to atoms. This has been known or suspected since the days of the Greeks Pythagoras, Leucippus, Epicurus, and the Roman Democritus, pupil of Epicurus, 2500 and more years ago.(1) And atoms are made of not a thing but negative and positive charges of electricity—electrons and protons. In the denser formations, the molecules are merely closer together than in the rarer ones. By the application of heat to solids, the molecules first have their attraction for one another reduced, then are forced apart by vibration, and they generally first become liquids and then gases. By the application of cold (which is nothing but a *lessening* of *heat)* to the fluids and gases, the vibration decreases, the molecules draw back nearer together, and they become liquids and solids."

"Everything that has life, whether animal or vegetable, is made up entirely of cells—each cell consisting of forty-eight parts. These cells are *electric cells*. In man there are close to 30 trillions of them. It follows that man—bodily, mentally, and spiritually—is electric."

"And what is an electric cell?"

"One type of inorganic cell is made up of a jar filled with a certain liquid, or electrolyte, having a piece of zinc at the top and copper at the bottom. The zinc terminal is the negative pole or electrode of the cell, the copper terminal the positive. At each pole a difference of potential exists between the fluid and the pole. Connect these two electrodes outside the jar by a wire and a current of electricity will flow. How does it flow within the liquid in the jar? Why, particles of the zinc, called ions (wanderers or travelers), are dissolved and pass between the poles carrying the current. The liquid around the positive plate or anode dissolves it; that around the cathode or negative releases hydrogen. This makes a difference of potential, which is what makes the current go. So long as it exists, the cell is operative—produces, or is capable of producing, current. When it ceases, the cell is dead—inoperative—can produce no current.

"Every one of the 28 to 30 trillion cells in a man's body is a prototype of this inorganic cell. There are the corresponding elements; there is the same mechanism for the production of a difference of potential; the same difference of potential; the same facilities for storing static electricity. So long as this difference of potential exists, the electricity, or biotic energy, called life is there—the man lives; when it ceases (that is say to when a positive acidity is established), the man dies—or, rather, is dead.

The electrical nature of life includes all such phenomena, as emotions, thought processes, memory and the like. And electricity being a material thing it follows that there is no immateriality. A thing is either material or it does not exist at all. Even energy is material, because matter goes directly into the making of it—it is transformed into it, and retransformed into matter. What we sometimes deem immateriality is merely a gradation upward beyond the range of our perceptions; but though it passes our perceptions it never passes materiality. Is there, then, no such thing as mind, soul, spirit? There is, by all means, but they, too, are material,(2) although of too rare a substance for our senses to cognize—a sort of particled, or disembodied matter, which is capable of freely permeating and traversing the solider forms.

"There are dense and rare media; some we can see and feel and some we cannot; but each medium is inhabited by its own distinct kind of organic, and perhaps sentient, creatures, varying with the necessities and limitations of their habitations. And as with the media, so with the inhabitants; some we can see and touch and become acquainted with; some we cannot, and remain in ignorance of."

HERE there was another sub-title, "Material Things Only By-products of Space."

"At first everything was gaseous, or at least of some rare consistence; then, in ways we are not wholly familiar with, whirls or eddies took place in these gaseous organizations, and after inconceivable periods became more condensed and solid—got to be what we call 'material things'—suns, planets, vegetation, animals.(3) But these are an infinitesimal part of the whole; merely the exceptional, and more or less casual by-products of space. They never were the important things; never concerned the real activity, which would continue though all 'material things' were dissolved.

"We are learning that the real activities of Nature are in what has been dismissed as 'empty space' and it is there scientists have gone to seek them. It is there the important acts go on, the vital things occur. Far from being 'empty' space is more vibrant and vital than the so-called 'material things.' The more tenuous things have assumed the major, the denser ones the minor roles.

"The laity still thinks the denser things the more real, and denies intelligence or consciousness to those more or less compact than themselves. Yet they themselves admit the mind or spirit to be the real thing, though itself as tenuous and elusive as the ether of space. Without it the body would be a dead nothing, and 'conscious existence' a myth.

"There is greater likelihood of mind existing in the rarer forms. The ether and the mind are closer kin; possess more homogeneous attributes; exhibit liker properties; are better fitted to deal with the kindred forces of magnetism, gravitation, light, space, time, and hence are more congenially companionate.

"The fact that some of this 'life' stuff is closely linked with animal bodies doesn't imply that all of it is. I have personally no doubt there are sentient, and probably reasoning, beings so rare we do not sense them at all."

Here Mansonby read with satisfaction, the title, "Elementals."

"An instance in point is the so-called 'elementals.' Their bodies are more tenuous than ours. The 'mass' contained in the body of an elemental a hundred feet in diameter is thought to be much less than that in the body of a man. And yet they are powerful. They are to some extent reasoning beings. They can choose one thing and refuse another. They remember and learn by experience. The stuff of which their *life* is made is the same stuff of which our *life* is made; for life, being an electric potential, is universal.

---

**(1)** It is probable the Greeks borrowed their atomic theories from the still more ancient Hindus.

**(2)** This is so far from being new or revolutionary that we find it laid down in the "Angutarra Nikara" of the ancient Hindus that mind or consciousness is atomic in structure.

**(3)** The reader may consult Plato's Timaeus, Aristotle's Metaphysica and Physica, De Anima and De Coelo, Diogenes Laertius's DeVitis, and many other ancients, all following the earlier Hindus. (Probably)

"Said Bouvier, 'There is nowhere any distinct break in the evolutionary series—no fundamental distinction between the animal and the human mind. Protoplasm is protoplasm, wherever found, and mind is mind wherever it becomes manifest. There can no more be two totally distinct and fundamentally different kinds of mind than there can be two or more totally distinct kinds of protoplasm, one human, the other sub-human. The Amoeba and Man are both the product of protoplasmic differentiation, and the primordial protoplasmic cell embodied in its substance all potentialities of Life and Mind upon this planet.'

"The elementals have been assumed by some to consist of disembodied matter, by which is meant, not any vague, metaphysical thing, but matter having its electrons and protons dissociated, so that they are no more matter in the ordinary sense than planets deprived of their sun would be a solar system.

"In order that readers may keep their minds clear, they are again reminded that in all matter, the electrons revolve about the protons, or nucleus, at enormous distances—compared with the size of the electrons themselves. Roughly, the diameter of the electron would bear about the same ratio to the diameter of its orbit as the diameter of the Earth to the orbit of the planet Neptune—or as one to 350,000. Therefore, vastly the greater part of the area between its orbit and the nucleus is empty space—space where there are no protons or electrons.

"APPLYING these facts to the body of a man, we find that only about one-billionth of a man is 'solid matter.' (The body of a man contains about 1081 electrons—10 followed by thirty ciphers). The remainder is space, and if this were eliminated by packing the electrons against the nucleus, several men could be placed inside a sphere the size of a pea, with plenty of room for their activities.

"If, then, an elemental a hundred feet in diameter contains less solid matter than a man, it must be rare indeed. Probably much less than one-trillionth of it is solid matter."

Sanderson's document continued: "Now during life there is always a certain electric potential in our bodies, which at times becomes an electric current. When light falls on the retina of the eye, an electric current is set up along the optic nerve. True, this bodily electricity is insufficient, with our present learning, with which to move our bodies about in space; but if we were as rare as the elementals, we might use it for motion through space by hooking up, as it were, with the electromotive force of the ether. Doubtless the elementals possess within their rarefied bodies the mechanism for this hook-up. Since, unfortunately, no elemental has been examined at close range, we can only speculate for the time being.

"We have laid too fast hold of the conception that a reasonable being must breathe the same air we do; be sensible to heat and cold in the same degree; have physical organs, forms, and attributes similar to our own; be subject to the same limitations of atmospheric pressure, gravity, and the like. But in truth, mind has little to do with these things.

"There would appear no logical argument against a gaseous creature as reasonable as we. Such a being would approach the ordinary conception of disembodied spirits or ghosts, its inexplicable colligations of gaseous atoms taking the place of our bones, muscles, and tissues. It would have the mental or spiritual element highly ascendant over the physical an (Query?) might explain phenomena relating to demonry, familiar spirits, its wizardry, moods, and the like. These things have usually appeared in epidemic or periodic surges, possibly corresponding with the unsuspected presence of such beings."

Mansonby finished reading, laid the manuscript on the desk before him, and looked inquiringly at Marlin.

"Good, isn't it?" he asked.

Marlin nodded after a moment. "If you like it, I'm for it, Chief. If it's an examination paper, let's see if the answers are in the back. There's a point or two I don't quite—"

Martin brought in Tardieux's pictures of the burned out remains of the strange creature. The negatives had been so clear that though greatly enlarged, the details were still visible.

Martin started to go out. "Have you a little time to spare, Martin?" asked Mansonby.

Martin hesitated. "Y-yes, Chief, if you need me; but I'll have to go first and give some directions to Hertzstein and Kung Foo Sze; then I can get away a while, I guess."

"Well, never mind right now; later will do. Have Ellis see if Ello-ta can come up, and if he can tell him to bring Mrs. Ello-ta and Miss Morrison."

Marlin had looked up suspiciously at the naming of the women, and reddened like a girl when Mansonby's glance flashed his way at the name of Miss Morrison.

Mary Terra Morrison was born on Jupiter; her father was Samuel Morrison, formerly of New York, who, many years before, with a party of other scientists, had been first to accomplish the dangerous crossing of the planetoid belt, between Mars and Jupiter. Unable to return on account of the accidental destruction of their vessel in landing (the facilities not being available to rebuild it), he had reconciled himself to the loss of his native Earth, married a Jovian woman—Mary Terra's mother—and settled down among the Jovians, where he had become respected and honored, and eventually elevated to the high position of head of the National House of Science, at Kalata (or Collata), the capital of the South Polar Region. He at once appointed as his assistant his fellow voyager, John Hudson, of San Francisco, California. Morrison's beautiful Jovian wife, Marela, he had called Mary, and when a daughter came, had named her for her mother, adding the name Terra in honor of his own native planet.

When Mansonby and his fleet of Tellurians and Martians had made their way to Jupiter to rescue the aged Cerean people, who had been carried away from their home on Ceres by the cruel half-beast, half-human Drugos of the Jovian Hot Lands, Morrison and Hudson were overjoyed at being reunited, after so many years, with members of their own race. During the engagement of the fleet on Jupiter, Mary Terra had formed so delightful a friendship with Signa Latourelle, the fascinating and piquant Adrienne, and the intelligent and interesting Therma Lawrence, that she had accepted their urgent invitation to return with them for a visit to her father's native world. During the trip to Earth, she had also become acquainted with Cyrus Marlin.

Of an unusually sweet and gentle nature, she had so endeared herself to her Terrestrian friends that they had steadfastly refused to listen to her leaving them. Adrienne, in particular had suggested—in her usual mischievous vein—that it was her duty to remain, because the big Marlin could so ill be spared by Mansonby. Whereupon Mary Terra had unblushingly declared Cyrus Marlin to be "the dearest big child on Earth or any other place," and Adrienne had responded with the injunction to grab him quick. "Because," she added, making a face at her husband, "if anything happened to Zah, I should marry Cyrus—which would be unpleasant for both you and him."

All of which would have woefully embarrassed the bashful Marlin if he had heard it.

It was precisely during this conversation that Ellis' summons had come, and the three prepared to go at once to the Interplanetary Building, Adrienne professing curiosity as to whether the present call was of martial or marital concern.

## CHAPTER FOUR

UPON their arrival Adrienne had danced gaily across the floor to plant a sisterly kiss on Mansonby's mouth, and then gone to offer her hand to Marlin—with such a devil in her eye that none but the innocent Marlin would have missed her sinister design.

"Mr. Marlin," she said reproachfully, standing close to him, "why do we not see you at our place? You haven't been—"

"Why, I'm sorry, Mrs. Ello-ta, but you know we have been so b-b-bus—"

It was done. Adrienne had planted a malicious kiss directly where it interfered most with Marlin's enunciation, much to his discomfiture. Then she made a face at her husband's fondly tolerant smile, hastily took possession of the chair in which Mary Terra was about to seat herself, forcing her to sit next to Marlin, and settled herself with profound gravity to listen.

Mansonby considered a moment before speaking. "Zah, I've called you here for several reasons."

"All falling, I presume," interjected the Cerean, "under the general head of elementals."

Mansonby gave him a look of pleased surprise and a nod. "My dear fellow, you're not at all dull, are you?"

"Oh no," agreed the Cerean, his intelligent face wearing a humorous half smile as he turned pointedly toward Adrienne and added "not anymore."

Whereas Adrienne arose to bow mockingly.

"And the women, Mansonby—I imagine you specified them in your invitation for reasons that—well—that we both understand."

Mansonby looked at the Cerean with frank admiration, and Marlin withdrew his eyes from Mary Terra to stare at him with equally frank bewilderment.

"On account," Ello-ta half stated, half explained, "of their possession of certain mysterious electric potentials, or mental qualities, that we men are not endowed with, and—"

Mansonby gave a little start, as at a new and pertinent idea.

"And," the Cerean continued, "because those qualities are likely to lend themselves very efficiently to our contest with beings against which our usual weapons would probably be of—er—little use. Well, Mansonby, old sleuth, you're intelligent, too. You've summoned the two for the job."

If Mansonby had been startled by the clear penetration of the Cerean, he was still further so at the words of the distractingly pretty, and usually light-hearted Adrienne.

"Yes, Mr. Mansonby," she said, "Zah is right. I do not quite see yet just how we shall act, but there can be no doubt as to the eventual unification of the thought power with the various other forces of Nature. Mary Terra and I have given much time and thought to our role. From long, and I may say, fairly successful experience with Zah in his telepathic experiments, we have developed certain forces to the point of some efficiency and discovered others we did not suspect we had—or anybody else. You gentlemen, proceed in your own way, and M. T. and I will work away in our way."

Mansonby nodded respectfully and turned to Ello-ta. "I don't suppose you have had access to an article of Sanderson's on the subject of—"

"Elementals? Oh, I have," interrupted the Cerean. "Adrienne picked it up in her omnivorous reading and brought it to my attention."

"Good. Then you might look at these pictures."

Ello-ta gave a half glance in their general direction and a lazy wave of the hand. "Tardieux's pictures? Yes. Interesting, aren't they?" He grinned humorously, with another almost imperceptible wave of the hand, at Mansonby's expression. "I procured copies by—a few minor perjuries—I procured copies, and—er—I've been most interested."

"Then I suppose you don't mind one more perjury, by admitting that you thoroughly understand them."

"Oh no," he replied, with one of his characteristic and favorite ambiguities. "I suppose my theories are about the same as yours—since they are the only tenable ones." His lips twitched as he added enigmatically, "with one or two exceptions. In fact," he went on after a second's pause, "I was going to furnish you a little Martian treatise of a very ancient date. I meant to bring it, but—I couldn't find it at the moment. Elementals, of course."

Adrienne fumbled in her bag, brought out the treatise in question, and offered it to her husband. "I—er—foresaw you would forget it, darling," she drawled languidly, "so I..." She finished with a perfect imitation of Ello-ta's indolent tone and wave.

There was a laugh all round, and Ello-ta put the packet on Mansonby's desk for future consideration.

Adrienne looked thoughtful and arose. "If you could excuse M. T. and me, Mr. Mansonby. Signa is about due in from Paris, as you know, and she's coming to our place about—something. And—" She hesitated in mock timidity, with a glance in Marlin's direction, "could you spare Mr. Marlin a few minutes to take us home? I know Zah won't be going for such a long while, and—I feel afraid. Some of those elemental things might—"

Mansonby, knowing full well that neither Adrienne nor "M. T." knew the meaning of fear, yet nodded slightly at Marlin. "Might as well get used to it, Marlin. And—take your time. Maybe you'd better stay and guard them till Zah gets back. We can't afford to lose them—not till this thing is over, anyway." Mansonby winked at Ello-ta, whose face continued as grave as a funeral.

Adrienne kissed her husband, whispered something in his ear, and the two girls went out, accompanied by the big Marlin. At the door they met Calder Sanderson and his wife. Sanderson remained, and Miss Lawrence excused herself to go with the two girls and Marlin.

Mansonby, Ello-ta, and Sanderson set themselves for a careful appraisal of the Tardieux pictures.

"Hmmm…tissue extremely rarefied," observed Ello-ta. "Looks like burned-out tissue paper honeycomb for all the world. Yes—lightning might do it." He pointed at the denser areas. "Short-circuited? Might be. Who can tell? Rarefied tissue just burned to nothing. I understand the greater part of the skeleton, if I may use that word, blew away with the first breeze."

Mansonby nodded. "Yes. That's correct. And you see these fibers passing round and round the skeleton, and connecting with the denser central parts?" He turned to Sanderson. "That bears out your theory?"

The scientist considered. "Possibly, possibly—or I may even say, probably."

Ello-ta clucked his tongue at Sanderson. "You're so rash, old fellow!"

They discussed the photographs for some time longer, and then Mansonby referred to Sanderson's article. "Did you have any particular scientific basis—any special authorities—for these extraordinary propositions you make, Professor? Or were you just—"

"Vaporizing? Oh no no… Most of it represents the conclusions of others than myself, from the ancient Hindus and Greeks, 3000 years ago, down to the present time." He was carelessly turning the pages as he spoke, "I see there is some little confusion here. I have said that all things are 'material,' and then seemed to draw a distinction between material and spiritual. I am afraid I used my words rather loosely."

"I understand. No, I think there is no real confusion, though a new vocabulary would be convenient in stating the matter. Now, since the elementals are mostly wind, we might say, what would be the effect of bombarding them with gunfire, in your opinion?"

Sanderson shook his head. "I do not know; but my guess is the effect would be to use up ammunition."

"And explosives?"

"Explosives? Well, explosives might blow them away a short distance, but the air rushing in to fill the momentary vacuum might draw them back where they were, and possibly—indeed probably—uninjured."

"Rays?"

"Heat rays they might be insensible to. Electric rays might—"

Mansonby turned to answer the ground phone. It was Marlin, and a very much perturbed Marlin—speaking from the Ello-ta home.

"Chief! For God's sake! Something terrible is happening! The women have gone crazy!"

"Crazy? Marlin, what are you talking about?"

FOR a moment there was silence, and Mansonby had about concluded the connection was broken. He tripped a small switch and connected the television. Upon the panel three feet by six at one side of his office flashed the strangest scene the three men had ever seen. Therma Lawrence lay on her face on the floor, weeping wildly, hysterically. Marlin was holding a fighting, kicking, struggling Mary Terra firmly with one arm, while striving to grasp Adrienne with the other. Adrienne evaded him agilely, her face a mask of indecipherable emotions. She was surely far from being her own gently mischievous self. Apparently Signa Latourelle had not yet arrived. As they gazed in stunned amazement, Adrienne, eluding Marlin's outstretched hand, made a mad dash for a window. With a mighty bound he was after her, catching her clothing barely in time to keep her from crashing through to the sidewalk, hundreds of feet below.

"For God's sake, *hurry*, Chief!" pleaded Marlin. "I can't keep this up forever. One of them will get away."

"Wh—what are you trying to do with them, Marlin?"

"Trying to *do?* I'm *trying* to keep them from jumping out of the window! They've all gone crazy, I tell you!"

As they watched, Adrienne suddenly sagged limply on Marlin's arm. Therma Lawrence, with a convulsive sob, relaxed and lay still; Mary Terra ceased fighting and lay quiet on Marlin's other arm. There were a few moments of dead silence, Marlin looking about helplessly. Then he carried Adrienne and Mary Terra bodily to a couch and lay Adrienne upon it, apparently unconscious. Mary Terra revived slightly and raised her head heavily, as if in a daze.

"Thank you, Cyrus, dear. I'm—I'll be—all right—now, I think."

The big detective helped her to a seat and released her grudgingly, watching her anxiously. "What's—are you sure you are—what was the—"

He turned to the television panel, breathing hard. "I think you had better hurry over here, Chief. I don't know what happened; but if it happens again I don't want to be alone with them."

"All right, Marlin, we're on our way." He cut off and rang for Martin. "Martin, get General Cohen, and ask him to call me at Mr. Ello-ta's at once," he flung back at him as he went out, and with Ello-ta and Sanderson, leaped into an aerocar and flashed away. Mansonby, at the controls, drove with a cool savagery that made his passengers gasp and reach hastily for solid holds. With a master hand he avoided the traffic, shooting like lightning above, diving sickeningly below, flashing to the right or left, avoiding collisions by magic, breaking every traffic law on the books. Once there was a light scraping as he flashed perilously between two aerocars, and a volley of curses from startled drivers followed them— so closely did Mansonby measure the inches between them and destruction. Several air police dashed sternly after them, but turned back on recognizing the car as belonging to the Mansonby Interplanetary. They made the twenty-seven miles in eight minutes under traffic conditions.

As they entered, Therma Lawrence was just recovering consciousness. Adrienne still lay quietly where Marlin had put her. Mary Terra and Marlin were standing near each other.

Ello-ta hurried to Adrienne.

"She'll be all right, Mr. Ello-ta," said Marlin gently. "I'd just let her lie quietly until she comes to."

When everything was straightened out Mansonby looked at Ello-ta and Sanderson with a meaningful glance, which they both received with a nod. Ello-ta spoke.

"Yes, Mansonby, you're right; but I suggest we conceal nothing from the women. They aren't the sort to faint over a mouse. They've been through a rather ghastly experience, and we have Marlin to thank for their lives. They'll want to know all about it."

But explanations proved quite unnecessary. The women realized as well as the men. They had been caught off guard by the malign, demoniac influence, which, on account of their marvelous sensitivity to thought-force, had driven them mad and forced them to do what they would have been the last to wish. At any rate, they were interrupted by the telephone. General Cohen was on. He had phoned Mansonby's office even as Martin was striving to get him and been put through. Evidently, although his voice was calm, he was having something of a time to keep it so.

"Mansonby? Why, Mansonby, one of my air guard in the five-mile level has just reported some strange object over this territory—a circular something of considerable size. And—get this! He says it is *alive*—an animal, not a ship. It seemed to be just hovering over—cruising back and forth. Personally I think the man's crazy, but of course it might be some foreign ether ship, and we can't afford to—"

"Yes. I know all about it, General. That's what I was calling you for. What measures have you taken?"

"You *know!* How *could* you know, Mansonby? The guard is out of sight above the clouds, and I only this moment got his message."

"Oh, the Interplanetary has ways of finding out things, General." Mansonby could not resist saying it, though he felt mean about it the next instant. "What measures have you taken?"

"Measures? Why none, Mansonby. What measures should I—I'm afraid I don't know precisely what you mean...measures?"

"Mean? I mean, General, that the answer to the problem you brought me has arrived and is now over New York. I mean the worst kind of hell is to pay. I'd advise you to order all aircraft down—in a hurry. Send out a general emergency, and see that it's obeyed *at once!*" This one your man saw is probably only a scout, and it means others will be along—probably very soon. I wouldn't tell the public too much; they might get panicky. I'd warn everybody to—no, it's not feasible to keep them all indoors yet, I suppose, without explaining why. They wouldn't stay. Well, tell them the police believe New York is threatened with an invasion from a mysterious foreign foe from The Outside, and that the danger is imminent and very grave indeed. If you don't feel like shouldering the responsibility for that, tell them I said so. Meantime we'll have to take the best measures we can to protect them. See that they keep out of the air. That's the main thing for the moment. All but the big ships. I think the big ships will be safe. I'm disconnecting so as not to delay you."

"Mansonby! Listen to me just a moment; will you? I chance, whether wisely or unwisely, to be the Chief of Police of the city and state of New York—a fairly responsible job. Something comes up that you seem to think is a grave menace. You suggest that I give drastic orders—orders that it will take every man I command to enforce. Do you think it is either wise or fair that I be kept in the dark as to—"

"No, I don't, General. I'm leaving for my office at once. I'll be there in fifteen minutes. Come right up and I'll tell you all I know. Meantime, if you don't feel like giving the order, I'll send it out myself, as an interplanetary officer whose orders the local police have no choice but to obey. There's not an instant to spare, General, but it's a poor place to go into details of this kind on the telephone. See you in fifteen minutes, then."

## CHAPTER FIVE

HE hung up without waiting for any further reply. Seating himself at a writing table, he took from a small folding pad in his pocket several official-looking sheets of paper and wrote thoughtfully for ten minutes, stopping occasionally to consider. At last, apparently satisfied with what he had written, he went and stood by a window with his hands clasped behind his back, his eyes seeing nothing of the gigantic city that stretched away out of sight in all directions below. Without turning, he asked Ello-ta to get through to his office and have them inform General Cohen that he would be a little late. While Ello-ta was complying with his request, he found an envelope and slipped the sheets of paper into it. Leaving it unsealed, he wrote something on it, took a pocket stamp from his pocket, and impressed it on the front and back of the envelope. The design showed an ether-ship, having a square cut into it bearing the words "Mansonby Interplanetary Service." It was the Mansonby insignia, known from one end to the other of the Solar System. The impress bore the additional words in small type, "This insignia is good for $100 at any Mansonby office if uncanceled." While this made it practically certain that any message bearing the stamp would be returned if lost or mislaid, it also made it necessary to guard the contents zealously and to cancel the stamp once its message was delivered.

Mansonby beckoned Marlin to one side and held out the envelope to him, showing him that it was unsealed. "Marlin, old man, will you get about this as quickly as you can, please? You will read this, of course. I'm sorry to put this on you, but—I don't like to trust it to anybody else."

The two conferred aside for some minutes in low tones before returning to the others.

"Take our car, Marlin," said Mansonby in dismissal. "We'll use one of Ello-ta's. And *fly low!* Right down close to the ground—and keep your eyes open. On no account venture higher than you are absolutely obliged to. All right, old chap, on the job, and good luck."

Marlin smiled and nodded at the others and turned to leave.

Mary Terra arose and went swiftly to put her hand on Mansonby's arm. "Please, Mr. Mansonby," she pleaded softly, "there's danger for Cyrus in this matter, I know— grave danger, isn't there? I feel it from your manner and his."

Mansonby patted her head fondly. "Why—my dear, I'm sorry, but—yes, there is always more or less danger in our business, but I wouldn't—"

The young girl gave a grim, resolute little nod and went to Cyrus Marlin. "Be careful, Cyrus—for your sake and mine," she pleaded. "I couldn't stand it to have—" Her tender lips quivered and her voice broke into a pitiful little sob.

It was too much. For once the bashful Marlin forgot to blush; for once he became masterful with a woman. Gently, reverently, he swung the little Jovian girl into his powerful arms and kissed the sweet, quivering lips. Her big, tear-flooded brown eyes closed while her arms strained about his neck.

"Don't be afraid, little one," he assured her tenderly. "Nothing to be worried about. I *will* be careful, though. Now I must hurry. You stay right with the Chief, and he'll take care of you." Another hurried caress and Cyrus Marlin had stepped into the Mansonby car, circled sharply and shot away into the west and out of sight.

Little did any one of the group suspect what lay right across the path of the brave, devoted Mansonby man. Nor would it have meant an instant's hesitation or wavering with Marlin had he known that he was to meet—that which he *was* to meet.

The people of Earth could not grasp the enormity of the ghastly menace that was upon them—which was not greatly to be marveled at.

The general emergency order sent out by the chief of police, and later broadcast to all Earth Detective Stations by Mansonby, created a veritable furor from the beginning. The tendency was to ignore it, and the forces available were far from sufficient to patrol the entire city and state and check the movements of all of the hundreds of thousands of aircraft that swarmed everywhere like bees. The more prudent and instinctively law-abiding at once assumed there was justification for the order or it would not have been given. These complied, if not unquestionably, at least with a fair degree of consistency. The second class who gave heed comprised those always-timid ones who not only fear to disobey any constituted authority but are afraid of even the shadow of danger. These, too, stayed out of the air. But far the greatest number either openly scoffed and ignored the order or put off compliance until the business in hand could be dispatched. Even if there was danger, business must go on. Money matters must not be jeopardized.

SOME of the press, though probably with the best of intentions, made the work more difficult. Eventually it cost many lives. To this class belonged such sheets as *The Daily Clarion, The Bugles, The Common People,* and others of that ilk. *The Clarion* carried a heavy black scare-headline across the front page of its morning edition: "OUR INDOMITABLE POLICE," followed by the only less glaring sub-heading, *"The Clarion* Scores Again." In just what manner *The Clarion* had scored was left a shade to the imagination. In part the story ran:

"As freely predicted by *The Clarion* at the time, the election of 'General' Ulysses Abraham Cohen as Chief of police two years ago is turning out a ludicrous blunder. Yesterday this remarkable man, without the slightest justification so far as we are aware, issued his imperial ukase, all wafered and sealed and done up in impressive bay ribbon, to the effect that henceforth all aircraft are to keep away from the air, under dire penalties. Somebody told him, it seems, that he had seen *an animal up in the air over the city.* Yes, dear reader, you heard correctly—an animal up in the air. Had it been the police who were alleged to be up in the air, one could perhaps understand and even applaud Cohen's auto-psycho-analysis. At any rate, he admits the police are very much afraid of this animal and think quite possible other sky animals may show up, causing them still greater fear. Meantime Cohen is petulant and ill natured because the people will not share his panic.

"For the first time in our memory, words entirely fail us. We seem to recall reading in our nursery days about a frolicsome beast that jumped over the moon, and it is of course just possible this is what is causing our worthy Chief of Police to tremble and his teeth to chatter so audibly. If so, we suggest that the milkmaid call her bossy down, slap her ears, and guard her more carefully in future. There is no predicting what dire disaster this humorous bovine might inflict on the minds of General Cohen and his intrepid men. We entreat our readers to be kind to the police and refrain from startling them by any sudden or unaccustomed sounds or movements."

There was more of the same sort, with bristling subtitles at strategic places. The people laughed over their breakfast coffee, toast, and eggs, and proceeded to fly to their business as usual. The police were a lot of boys—quite comical. It might be well for the Commissioners to put the juvenile traffic squad in charge of the situation until the police recovered from their scare.

The afternoon edition of this same *Clarion* ran a black headline, "COWS COMING HOME," and a smaller one, "Cohen Thinks Whole Herd Taken to Air." And a still smaller one, "Great Excitement among Police. Citizens Warned against Cow Bites."

*The Defendant* and the *Common People* vied with the bigger *Clarion* in a perfect riot of ridicule against the hard-working peace officers. The former included "the aristocratic and undoubtedly powerful Mansonby" in the general arraignment, and the latter shed inky tears that even the Department of National Defense had allowed itself to be so far stampeded by the police as to endorse Cohen's hysterical order and lend a considerable fleet of aircraft to its enforcement.

Of the more conservative press, one jocularly remarked that it appeared to be "a political play and might be fairly charged to the party beaten at the last election." Another humorously asserted its conviction that the whole alarm was a publicity stunt "arranged by the Farmer Party with a view to recommending itself for the relief it has so long sought in vain." Others reminded the people soberly that whatever the "yellow press" might say the sensible element would hesitate about disobeying an order that was endorsed by "the able Cohen and Mansonby, to say nothing of the department of National Defense."

*The Clarion's* reply was an immediate extra, proclaiming that the editor of that paper would, on the morrow at noon, enter his aerocar in Times Square and proceed to chase the offending sky animal to some place where it would not frighten the police. Enormous numbers of the edition were scattered broadcast, free to whomever would take them, and placards were posted in large letters at the most public places in the city, "Remember, people, at Noon Tomorrow! Be there! See the Great Show! If the sky-animal is not too fleet for our aerocar, the editor will endeavor to present the police with a steak cut from the sky-cow."

The announcement made a tremendous hit, and the subsequent extras of *The Clarion* that day sold faster than the presses could produce them.

But alas for the editor of *The Clarion*, at the hour set with so great éclat for his heroic feat, the morning sun saw a dozen of the beasts hovering almost directly over Times Square, and the hour of eleven saw that number doubled. It would almost appear as if the creatures had read the posters and gathered themselves to see what would happen.

The noon edition of *The Clarion*, industriously distributed everywhere, announced with extreme regret that the editor had gone to the hospital to be operated on for a sudden acute attack of appendicitis, but promised in loud tones that as soon as he should recover the flight would positively be made as announced.

The next edition was laughed off the streets.

IN Mansonby's office and among his coterie of immediate friends there was great anxiety over Marlin in the weeks that followed. The matter on which he was engaged had necessitated that he go to more distant points than had been expected. On the second day after his hurried leave—taking he had communicated with Mansonby from St. Louis—he was leaving for farther west points. On the third day a garbled message had been received from him, which was broken off in the middle either by faulty transmission conditions (it was evidently being sent by Marlin with a pocket transmitter) or by some circumstances which, remained purely a matter of conjecture. Since that time nothing had been heard from him, and constant inquiry at all points, where it was thought he might have been seen, failed to elicit any information concerning him. He had not arrived at San Francisco or Los Angeles, at both of which points he had expected to call.

To make matters worse, the psychic Mary Terra awoke one morning from a restless and miserable night with the clear impression of a message seared into her brain. She declared that her lover was in desperate danger and himself almost in despair as to the outcome. For several succeeding nights she would start out of her sleep with the same nightmarish obsession. She was unable to shake off her depression and apprehension and became almost ill as a result. It seemed to take all of her strong will to keep up. She would have taken an aerocar and gone at once in search of Marlin, but Mansonby assured her he had already taken every possible measure to find him, taking airships away from other work to comb every mile of the western country, equipped with all known weapons of search, including telepathy. And seeing the stark misery in Mansonby's eyes, there was no doubting that all would be done that could be done.

And so it was with heavily burdened hearts that the little inner circle of the Mansonby Interplanetary carried on during the succeeding weeks, as the searchers reported continued failure. Mary Terra's messages had ceased abruptly, and she declared he was either dead or safe. As the weeks accumulated into months, it began to look as if they were never to see him again.

The appearance of the enemy scout had been quickly followed by others. At first there were only a few scouts, merely cruising here and there, in groups of two or three, over the different centers of population. They were cloudily semi-transparent by day, luminous with a pallid, ghastly phosphorescence by night. They had the appearance of merely scouting about pending the arrival of a greater force.

The combined forces of the police and defense departments, supplemented by every resource of the mighty, far-flung Mansonby Interplanetary, did not suffice to keep the people obedient to the sweeping orders that General Cohen had sent out after his telephone conversation with Mansonby at the Ello-ta home. The human being will never believe others. He must see for himself—an admirable trait, albeit often disastrous. Living themselves on a mere grain of cosmic sand, knowing almost nothing of what goes on in the great universe, they yet assume and insist that such and such things *cannot be*.

It was impossible to put the whole country into jail for disobedience. A number of the offenders, taken here and there to show that the police meant business, already crowded to overflowing all available places of detention. These were imprisoned for a day, or a day and a night at the most, given a "good talking to," and upon promising future obedience, turned loose with a warning.

Many probably knew nothing about the orders. Incredible as it may seem, there were still many who had not been willing to spend the few paltry pennies that would have put radio appliances into their homes, or even the still smaller sum to supply themselves with old style telephones. There was no way to reach and warn such, as all mail deliveries had been suspended.

Many laughed at "the whole ridiculous business." In general, the more they were warned, the less they heeded. The like had never been heard of and it was outside their experience or belief. Such fantastic creatures as the police were trying to frighten them with were simply absurd. There could not be intelligent living beings of any such sort. The prevalent verdict was that there was no such animal. They would assuredly, have known it before if there had been. Did the police think they were children to run into the house and hide in a closet, just because something or other had blundered accidentally into their atmosphere?

So they laughed and went about the business of making a little more money. An aerocar would be flying along; an automobile on the highway; men at work in the fields; women and children on picnics; groups of people here and there—then a swift, soundless swoop from above, the suffocating embrace of the creatures of their unbelief, and that was the end for the men, women and children. The people were literally "gobbled up" by the thousands as the number of the enemy increased during the succeeding weeks.

The larger ships were not molested at first, the intelligent creatures evidently either realizing that the big craft were too much for them, or else awaiting the time when easier prey should be lacking.

Over the United States the sinister dragons of the ether, in ever-multiplying numbers, hovered and dived, wheeled and dived again and again, ghostly, foul, nauseous; and each time, human beings or animals passed into the ravening maws.

Slowly, stubbornly, realization came to the populace as the detestable hordes overspread the Earth and a mad panic set in, which reached its remotest corners. All races, colors, and conditions alike—such as were left of them—began to mill about in frantic terror. If it had at first been difficult to coax or browbeat them to do anything in the way of taking precautions, it was now impossible to get them to do anything but skulk in their homes, or whatever places seemed to offer them the most security from the primordial menace.

The police, armies, and navies of the whole Earth riddled the mysterious creatures with millions of bullets and shells from the guns of the airships—in vain, as Sanderson had predicted. Some were shattered in vital parts, and brought down, but for the greater part they remained unharmed. A hundred bullets flung into one of them had little more effect than sticking pins into jelly. Such specimens as were secured the scientists experimented with, dissected, analyzed, tested, and talked about, and reduced their findings to copious nothings; but nothing was established that had not already been known or suspected. The learned doctors of science could offer no means for their destruction.

The rare, unchemical tissues of which they were made would yield to none of the known treatments. All they knew was that electricity reduced them to delicate ashes.

Again and again vast fleets of airships rained down into their midst torrents of high explosives. Most of these the elementals dodged, but when they did not, the only result produced was what Sanderson had also foretold—they were brushed aside, only to return on the back-wash of air into the vacuum. The atmosphere was tortured with seething clouds of poisonous, corrosive, and fiery gases. A dozen assorted kinds of deadly rays were played upon the masses. Some of these were effective, but after a few lessons the creatures nullified these temporary successes by flying too high and shifting their attacks to the nighttime or to places where they seemed to sense that defense was lacking. In other words, they simply dodged the attacks, and their lightning speed enabled them to do this effectively.

## CHAPTER SIX

WHILE the people had roamed about more or less freely, the invaders were content to take their toll wherever and whenever they could get them. There were enough thousands to be picked up for their needs, it seemed. But as the people became stricken with panic, and remained more and more indoors or under protection, they could not come at them. Necessary traveling was done by railway, or by air or water ships of a size that the creatures could not destroy.

The number of the attackers was augmenting constantly. Where there had been scores or hundreds, there were now dense masses, and over the centers of population they hung in clouds. This meant that their demand for food increased enormously. They could not enter the houses to take their prey. They must bring their prey to them; and in how monstrous and unthinkable a manner they did this will be seen.

Mansonby had not failed to learn the true lesson from the destruction of the first elemental by lightning in France. He had argued from the beginning that electricity was the only thing that would destroy the sinister visitants. Such great concerns as the Tellurian Electric Company, the Westinghouse, the Edison Universal, the German Interplanetary, and a host of others of all nations had early come forward and placed their entire resources at his disposal. Preparations had been made to project against the enemy, bolts of artificial lightning of many million volts.

But after several months of arduous preparation and the expenditure of enormous sums, this method was quickly shown to be nearly useless—certainly nothing like adequate to give any permanent relief. Here and there numbers of the creatures were brought down and became ashes that blew away on the first breeze. But the lightning bolts were available only in clear weather. When clouds were in the sky, attackers stayed above them, and the lightning reached only to the clouds and no farther. Many times the clouds, becoming surcharged, shot back real lightning along the line of the artificial, with fatal consequences to the senders.

And, too, the elementals learned quickly. During clear weather they kept out of range and attacked only in the darkness, which their sense of sight—whatever that was—seemed to penetrate as well as the light. In cloudy weather they massed above the clouds, and swooped swiftly when they saw anything to devour. The fields and ranges were speedily decimated of livestock, until it seemed as if domestic

The fields and range were decimated of livestock

Arctic, the bears, reindeer, seals, and like creatures, were soon unobtainable, even had the terrified people dared to go out to find them. Usually they preferred to starve rather than face the prospect of themselves becoming food.

In such densely populated centers as India and China, the daily victims were numbered by the hundreds of thousands. There was no protection for these, no shelter to which they could retire and be safe. Fishermen were swept off the seas. Something must be done, or the world would die of starvation.

The forces of the Earth were divided into offensive and defensive, the former devoting their attention to trying to drive away or destroy the hordes, the latter to devising all possible ways of keeping their victims from them. Many defensive expedients were tried in the cities first. Chief of these consisted of stringing copper

animals were to become extinct from the Earth. In the outland regions, where the people depended largely on animals for food, starvation began to draw nearer and nearer. In the

173

wires over the streets, a few feet apart, and charging them heavily with electric potential. This had some success, and was extended to some of the agricultural lands. But there was neither enough wire to protect large areas, nor enough power in the demoralized condition of things to charge them. And there was the difficulty that every time the enemy swept down upon them, the wires were dragged to the ground and rendered useless until extensive repairs could be made; and the elementals, as if realizing the difficulty, hovered over the very sections where necessary work was in progress. Then steel rails were elevated on supports a few feet above the ground, and the wires strung on them. This succeeded to such an extent that agriculture began to be carried on over larger and larger regions, and the people in the protected areas regained a measure of their former freedom. But it was impossible to

fortify the whole world in that manner. In such countries as Africa and the outlying regions of South America, the population, both human and brutes, almost disappeared, becoming prey either to the elementals or to starvation.

It had become a struggle whether the Earth should continue to be the abode of the human race, or become the home of these weird phantoms of space.

In this manner a year passed. In that time it was estimated (although admittedly it was only a guess) that of the population of eight billion on Earth, a third had gone to feed the clamorous hunger of the demons of space.

To make matters worse, it began to be apparent that a gradual but sure deterioration in the mental and moral fiber of the people was setting in. At first it was not very marked, and none could say it was anything more than the natural outcome of the continually strain of anxiety and fear, accentuated by the lack of proper food. But instead of getting better it grew steadily worse, until it was impossible longer to doubt its true cause. Unaccountable things happened continually. The days were ridden with a strange madness, the nights peopled with profound and unnamable terrors. The reason of the Earth seemed tottering to its fall— the mind of man was turning to water. Was man—Great Man in the image of God—to go down into utter damnation and ruin? Was this noblest animal of all creation to be unable to extricate himself from the grip of the hovering terrors?

HOW many times during the ages, usually in idle speculation or jest, had the question been variously asked: Suppose some sinister things of which we have no conception, all unsuspected, were watching us, awaiting their moment to descend and sweep us from our precarious perch on the Earth? May not some terror be hovering near us even now, watching as we sleep at night, as we arise to the day, as we go about our work or our play? How can we know that some hideous aerial monster is not waiting for the time which it shall deem ripe, to swarm over puny man and destroy him utterly?

The Thing, the Terror, the Monster, had come to make answer, and Mighty Man had yet found no way of beating it back.

When it was noised about that the cities had devised ways of protecting themselves, the country took its hands from the plow, threw down its hoes and shovels, and flocked to the cities as fast as they could find airships to take them, or the intervening highways were placed under the electric protection. But wherever people are, they must find means of stoking their thirty billion minute electric cells, lest a positive acidity being established, the electric potential called "life" be destroyed. And food was already insufficient for all. True that the airships could still go where they would without any great peril; the railroad trains could do the same; the ships could still sail the seas. But wherefore? Where should they take their passengers? The great quest was for food, and there was the same dearth of it wherever they could go. They could fish from the big ships, and did, but the fishing grounds soon were depleted.

The Interplanetary fleets carried such as cared to go to other planets, only to find that they would have been as well or better off at home. By this time every inhabited planet in the Solar System (and every uninhabited one, too, so far as anyone could say) was blanketed with the unhallowed scourge. Interplanetary travelers reported the elementals swarming everywhere throughout space. It seemed as if the whole cavernous hells of the limitless void were vomiting their grisly contents upon the human race to harry them out of being. It seemed as if the painfully erected civilization of the centuries, with all of its complicated modern life, was to be a dead and gone thing of the past. Where did this abysmal swarm of ghouls come from? One could not say. What had caused it suddenly to break away from its far home and descend like an unholy avalanche upon humanity? One did not know. Had they spawned and grown in the fiery regions of the outer planets of our own system—Saturn, Uranus, Neptune, or that other yet unnamed planet outside the orbit of Neptune? Or did they come from some mysterious and unknown distant region of space? Nobody knew—likely both. The one thing that was becoming apparent to all alike was that unless some effective means was found to eliminate them, and quickly, the human race was to vanish, and the millions of years of evolution would be flung away and have to be done all over again.

In Mansonby's offices there was definite mourning. Marlin had not returned and had long been given up for dead. Although desolated over their loss—for Marlin, like his chief, had been universally loved—Mansonby and his people must carry on as best they could. Mary Terra bore up heroically, and with Adrienne, Signa, and Therma and other women carefully sought out and chosen for certain mental potentialities, labored unceasingly night and day with Ello-ta and Sanderson at some abstruse experiments that never seemed to come either to flower or fruition.

Upon Jupiter there had at first been some success under the leadership of Maltapa Tal-na and Rala, the Jovian War Chief. For several months the Jovians suffered little. But this turned out to be rather from circumstances than any real ability to cope with the enemy. The elementals had occupied themselves at first with the Vulnos—the Drugos and the Guvolus—of the Hot Lands, leaving the civilized population of the north and south polar regions largely in peace. But after the prey to be had for the taking in the Hot Lands had been exhausted, the elementals widened the scope of their hunting into the polar regions. Just as the Jovians needed his help the most sorely, Maltapa Tal-na was hurriedly recalled home. Mars, for some unknown reason the last planet to be visited, was not suffering with the rest. In fact, Mars and Earth were the most vulnerable from their drier climate and less luxuriant vegetation. On Jupiter; Venus, and Mercury the forests foiled the elementals; they could not solve them. Moreover, the people were to a great extent vegetarians, and edible vegetation was everywhere so abundant · that there was little danger of hunger, and when the people had learned to keep where the elementals could not come at them, they did very well.

Mansonby was in constant touch with all of the planets of the Solar System, exchanging views and experiences, so that every method that promised any success in one world was tried in the others. As never before, the whole Solar System was welded together as one, with a common danger and a common purpose to escape it if they might.

In this manner the second year passed. There had been temporary successes against the elementals in various places and by various methods. At times there had seemed hope, but each time the successes were countered by some new move of the spectral visitants with a cleverness and resourcefulness that was remarkable.

Meantime, though there had been no return of the violent and overwhelming experiences of Mary Terra, Adrienne, and Therma Lawrence, the mental fiber of the people was steadily becoming more flaccid and inert. Mansonby and all of his immediate party had felt sure at the time that the mental symptoms of the women were caused in some manner by the elementals; but with the continued immunity from that phase of attack, this had begun to be doubted, and had been practically dismissed from most minds before this later epidemic of decadence set in. Mansonby almost alone had reserved his judgment and filed the matter away in his encyclopedic mind for future reference. Now, although he stated his conclusions openly, the people would not believe.

Nor will it be supposed that the Mansonby forces were immune from the general decimation during the terrible two years. Wherever there was danger, there the devoted men of the Mansonby Interplanetary were found in the middle of the transaction. Composed of individuals of every civilized nation of the Earth, as well as representatives from every planet, they laid down their lives freely when duty demanded, with no regard for any lines of color, nationality, or condition. Mansonby had a way with his men that made them face danger and death cheerfully for him, as they knew he had always done for them.

ONE of the most heroic acts of the entire elemental siege was performed by a Japanese member of Mansonby's organization. A special railway train, containing fifty

Mansonby men, had been wrecked in the middle of the Great American Desert. Thirteen had been killed, and the survivors were cooped up in the train, escape from which was cut off by a large number of elementals hovering persistently near. They seemed to know there had been a disaster, and like scavenger birds were awaiting the moment when their prey would fall into their maws. There was food for only a few days. The wreck lay many miles from assistance. Of all the multitudes of airships of sufficient size, not one was available at the moment to go to the rescue. As if in league with the enemy, a heavy storm had come up, washing out the railroad tracks on both sides of the beleaguered party. To escape from the wreck would have meant walking many miles. The only means of rescue available were small aerocars.

Yamamoto, a Japanese attached to Mansonby's New York office, but then in San Francisco, volunteered to lead a party in an attempt to effect a rescue. In the press of a thousand other duties, Mansonby was compelled to leave the matter to his representative in San Francisco, who, himself beset by other demands, was glad to yield to the request of Yamamoto to be allowed to make up his own party. With a party of twenty-five Japanese and Chinese, Yamamoto set out at night with twenty-five aerocars.

They reached the wreck in a few hours without interference, took the survivors of the wreck into their cars, and were about to leave the scene when a swarm of elementals swept overhead and awaited developments. It was a situation of sufficient desperation. The only thing the relief expedition had accomplished, apparently, was to add to the number of the marooned party, and hence to the difficulty of the situation. But the brave Japanese remained smilingly unperturbed. In a detached and casual manner he lighted a cigarette and puffed a moment with a thoughtful relish.

"Mr. Watson," he said at length to the leader of the whites, "I make you a sporting proposition. I have twenty-five men with me; you have thirty-seven with you. There is enough car room for all. I will load my men into one squadron; you load yours into another. I will take off a few minutes in advance of you. Possibly the elementals will follow us; possibly they will not; I do not know what they will do. If they follow us, I think we can keep them engaged for a few minutes before..." The Japanese paused with a grin on his swarthy face, "...well, before anything much happens. We ought to be able to give you five minutes—possibly ten or fifteen minutes' start. You will fly in the opposite direction, and with luck—well, with enough luck, you have a chance. What do you say, Mr. Watson? If they follow us, you can escape; if they do not follow us, we can escape. It is fair, is it not?"

Watson wrung the hand of the brave Nipponese. "Yamamoto, you're the bravest man I ever saw. But I shall not permit you to make any such sacrifice. I make the counter proposition that some of your men and some of mine ride in each aerocar; that we take off at the same time in as many different directions as there are aerocars. Some of us may win through, in which event some of us will be saved and some of you."

The Japanese shook his head vigorously. "You do not understand my plan, Mr. Watson. I have the advantage of having fewer men, and I have a plan, and you must please let me work it out. But I think you have added a good idea. My squadron will spread out in a fanlike formation, each car taking a different direction, but all generally eastward. This will give us a better chance to—to do what I have in mind. It is dark yet. That may be in our favor...maybe not so much. At any rate, it *seems* safer. You must not wait too long but long enough. It will depend. You will have to decide that.

But when you do start, have each plane take a different route, but all toward the Pacific. That way some of you may get away, maybe all. Ready, Mr. Watson! Fly low and—good luck. My greetings to the Chief."

The two men clasped hands again; Yamamoto sang out an order to his men, who quickly sprang to their places, and at his signal flashed away to the east, spreading apart as they went. With a wave and a smile the Japanese Mansonby-man followed.

At first the elementals did not appear to notice their departure. Their vaguely luminous shapes continued to ride like slow ghosts overhead—silent, gruesome, horrible. Perhaps they were asleep—if such creatures sleep. Suddenly one of them darted off in pursuit and the others shot after with a speed that boded no good for the Japanese and Chinese, who were crowding on every ounce of power their machines were capable of.

Watson waited until pursued and pursuers had passed over a low range of hills a few miles away, then he ordered his men into the air. Every man of them got away, but not a single one of the Orientals was ever seen or heard of again. They had gone cheerfully to the most horrible death imaginable. But that was the way with the Mansonby-men.

Long afterward, when next he saw the Chief, Watson did not fail to repeat to him the last words of the devoted Yamamoto, "My greetings to the Chief." Nor did he fail to hand him a note the Japanese had slipped into his pocket, which said: "Dear Watson, You are thirty-seven Mansonby-men; I am only one and the rest of my crowd are just pick-ups who could handle a car. Surely the Chief can do more with your thirty-seven than with me."

Other examples of sublime heroism were not wanting. All national lines were obliterated, and the world became one against the horde that seemed to promise the extinction of man.

# CHAPTER SEVEN

MEANTIME Ello-ta was working night and day with Professor Sanderson and their assistants on his telepathic theories. Many who knew of his efforts scoffed. It was absurd! Ridiculous! The *mind* sent out no waves, or vibrations, or current of any kind. Why, the mind was not a *material substance!* A thought was not a *thing!* The mind worked inside the head—the brain. Ello-ta's ideas about reading people's minds were comical. They were merely— well, what was the use of talking about such nonsense?

Others, while wishing to be fair, still found the thing too far beyond them and had serious doubts. It might possibly be true, though unlikely. Very unlikely indeed. On the face of it, Ello-ta had given some remarkable demonstrations— though perhaps hardly demonstrations. "Mind reading" had been claimed for centuries and usually been exposed in the end as mere trickery—skullduggery. If Ello-ta's results were not that, and to be fair he did not appear a trickster, well, there were exceptional minds. Probably his was one of them. That might account for it. Ello-ta was a rather remarkable person, to be sure.

Few seriously believed much, if anything, would be accomplished. Suppose he *could* read people's minds? He could hardly expect to read the minds of the elementals, if they had any. And even if it was admitted that he could read their minds (if they had minds, which was unlikely), and even if he could communicate with them, which of course was impossible, what good could it possibly do? Did he expect to coax or argue or wheedle them into going away?

And so it went. Ello-ta neither knew nor cared about the people's opinions. Mansonby knew; Sanderson knew. They knew what he had been doing and what he was now attempting. Mansonby had been here and there about the Solar System, poking into odd out-of-the-way places and seeing unbelievable things, until he was willing to admit the possibility of almost anything.

All these doubtings and scoffings were directly in the face of the fact—as will be remembered by those who have read "The Cry from the Ether"—that Ello-ta had rendered valuable aid at the most critical stage of the adventure through the medium of his telepathy. His ability to pick up and interpret, to some extent, even though imperfectly, the thought currents from the minds of the Cereans, had shown the way to their hiding place and resulted in their rescue by a hair's breadth from the savage Drugos of the Hot Lands. But that accomplishment had been too far away for the people of Earth to credit. Probably coincidence. People must have things under their noses to believe.

Since the appearance of the elementals on Earth, the eminent scientist, Sanderson, had added the entire weight of his great learning and resources to Ello-ta's efforts.

Their immediate quest was a means of magnifying and intensifying what might be called the electromotive power of the infinitely delicate waves that emanate from the human brain as thought to the point where they would become a dynamic, driving *force*. Mansonby's two chief reliances had been electricity and telepathy. The former had been rendered nugatory by its own limitations and the cleverness of the enemy. Now it seemed as if the sole remaining hope of escape from the encompassing doom lay in this delicate creation of science.

Ello-ta's reasoning, in which Mansonby and Sanderson had concurred, had been in this vein: A sound inaudible to the unaided ear could, by proper appliances, be magnified or amplified into a thunderous roar; a light of low candle power could by reflection and re-reflection be intensified into a blinding glare; the force of gravity could be increased or diminished at will; and an electric potential could be stepped up or down as desired by the use of transformers. Why, then, should not thought waves, close kindred to those of sound, light, gravity, and electro-magnetism, be capable of the same amplification? He believed they were susceptible to it, if he could only find the secret.

After discouraging failures he had noticed one day in experimenting with a delicate mechanism, more delicate than even the thermo-couple, that a sustained mental impulse, directed by a usage of telepathy he had already perfected, affected the mechanism. By repeated tests he found he could produce this effect at will, and felt he was at last getting near to what he was after. Calling in Adrienne and Mary Terra, who held themselves constantly at his orders, he found that they could produce the phenomena more efficiently than he. This was superior to any results previously accomplished. It was a direct and immediate controlling of matter by mental force alone.

Why not, he asked himself? There never had been any doubt about the control of matter *in some manner* by mind. There never had been any disputing of the fact that there was some point of contact between mind and matter, where mind took hold of matter and swung it this way, that way, or the other, at will. Every time a word was spoken, mind controlled matter; every time a human motion was made, mind controlled matter. The mind *willed* speech or movement, gave the command, and matter obeyed. The fact that the mind had some control over matter never had been open to doubt.

But the way the mind did this had been a "mystery," and it had at last come to be supposed it always would remain a mystery. Doubtless it might have, if certain masterminds had not gradually paved the approach by unifying the various natural forces into a single homogeneous whole; showing they were but parts of attributes or phases of one and the same thing. First "time" had been definitely removed from the misnomer "fourth dimension" and reconciled and unified with the known physical laws of the three dimensions. Then "space" had been joined with time and added to the harmony. Then electro-magnetism had been included, and afterward gravity had been shown to be a sort of twin sister to electro-magnetism. These great minds had shown the way to such a correlative understanding of the forces of Nature as linked them all into one cohesive and coherent whole. Old laws were upset and had to be discarded for new ones. "Energy" had been proven to be "material"—to possess weight and to obey the same laws as other matter. Matter was transmuted into energy and energy back into matter. In short, everything was being reduced to a single electrical unity.

Then WHY, asked Ello-ta, should "mind" itself, electrical like the others, be the only thing to stand outside the fold? Why should not mental force be brought into relation? Why should it not be possible to place the finger of science upon the precise spot and manner of the interaction of mind and matter and then to scrutinize that spot and find out what took place there? If two dead rocks could affect each other and draw together through gravity, why should not two living minds be able to do as much?

This Ello-ta believed he was on the way to accomplish.

All of which appeared at a great distance from the subject in hand—the destruction or repulse of the elementals. It resulted in a verdict from a considerable jury, including Ventrosino, at the Major Observatory, that Ello-ta was—an ass!

Meanwhile, as time went on, the victims of the elementals became fewer and fewer. It appeared as if they had exhausted the ready supply. Through the efforts of Mansonby, aided by the police, and the Department of National Defense, much had been accomplished in the way of protecting the people and permitting them to go about their business (even if on a half-filled stomach) of rehabilitating the world's food supply. Great Man was not quite helpless. He was not minded to go down without a fight. Great Man could will things, and they were brought into solid being. Besides, Great Man did not wish to die.

IN the cities the people had become comparatively safe from the gruesome hordes that hovered always above them. There, business began to go on much as usual and might have done so indefinitely but for the vital necessity of more food, which is not much produced in cities. It is true that by the time matters had simmered down, less food was needed to feed the world, because the population had been reduced by such an appalling fraction. Less food was required, certainly. But even so, there was not enough. The whole world was on short rations, which were becoming shorter. Agriculture had been extended, gradually, laboriously, under the electric protection, with many reverses and disasters; and eventually there were crops again—but not enough. Arrangements were under way to obtain vegetable food from Venus, where it was plentiful, but it had not yet begun to come through. As for meat, it had passed out of the diet of the people (many thought better so). What food animals had escaped the general destruction were being saved for breeding against the time when protection could be afforded them in numbers again. Severe laws were passed against the killing of any food animal. Most of the others remaining alive had been killed to save them suffering, since there was no food for them. Eventually the spectral enemy might have been starved out and gone away. This had come to be the main hope of many.

But the elementals did not go away. They had not yet fully extended themselves it seemed, not yet exhausted their resources, as was soon to be manifest. These willful, elusive humans must be taught other lessons yet. They must be taught *to come to them! Ridiculous!* Great Man would have said. But was it? These were *elemental creatures.* They were not physical as men are physical. They were less physical; had more of the primordial mental stuff.

At this stage of affairs strange things began to be noticed—strange and unaccountable mental abnormalities and maladies. People were taken by mysterious possessions, ghostly obsessions, weird feelings of spectral presences. Violence increased, running often to insanity, fanaticism, and general irresponsibility. The hand of Cain was raised on the Earth. Riots broke out without apparent cause, and there was a mounting tide of robberies, murders, rapine, and other crimes. The jails and asylums were filled to capacity, and there was no place for the overflow, which must be left to run riot, destroying and being destroyed.

It was noticeable that these crimes were not limited, even chiefly, to the ordinarily criminal classes. Ministers in their pulpits—men of blameless lives—abruptly swung from the exposition of the gospel to grotesque and indelicate rantings. Grave, staid professors suddenly forgot their subjects to run amuck among the members of their classes, gibbering wild inanities, mouthing meaningless drivel, assaulting their pupils. And the pupils joined the frenzied melee. Those of intellectual attainments fell the more readily under the strange spells; those of sluggish mentality and younger children were usually immune.

Bedlam broke loose, and confusion became worse confounded. Hardheaded businessmen rushed forth from their offices and counting-houses; laborers abandoned their work; policemen left their beats. There was a tendency to run madly about, without any regard to protection or safety. And again, here and there and everywhere, there would be the silent swoop from above and—the insatiable maws were filled again.

The sane ones were compelled to forsake every useful task and help restrain and care for the mad ones. Business was neglected; traffic jammed the ways in inextricable confusion; agriculture, which had begun to look up, dwindled again. All schools, churches, and other public institutions had to be closed. The elementals had re-established their ascendency, and the population began to decrease. Swarms of the hideous attackers edged down closer and closer, bolder and bolder, darting swiftly here and there like obscene ghosts, to seize any exposed ones and rise to do the like again and again. The atmosphere took on an unclean dankness, as of the tomb, as the creatures swirled in undulating waves, like the indomitable surges of some infernal sea, about to engulf the little island in space on which the Tellurians lived. It seemed as if they were impatiently determined to make an end to these humans and establish themselves as the lords of the worlds once for all.

Mansonby's forces suffered severely because of their general refusal to forsake their duties. The Mansonby men were like that. They consented to be killed, but refused to be daunted. Owing to the vital importance of keeping his organization functioning, Mansonby had concentrated his immediate friends, assistants, and employees in the Interplanetary Building for greater impactness and safety. They worked, ate, slept, and lived there, going out only when it could not be avoided, and then keeping under protection.

# CHAPTER EIGHT

IT was as the second year of the invasion was just drawing to a close that the disaster overtook the Martian Flier Ship *"Therma,"* named in honor of his daughter by Octavus Lawrence, the Interplanetary financial wizard, who owned the line. She was on the way out from Venus to Earth, loaded to capacity with passengers, the reported number being 6,164, besides her crew of 397, and a heavy first cargo of foodstuffs. More than half of the passengers were Venerian scientists, operatives, and various skilled technicians, on the way to lend their assistance to Earth and Mars. Many of them were Mansonby men (the roster of persons directly and indirectly in the employ of the Mansonby Interplanetary was said to number around 4,500,000). By this time Venus and Jupiter had brought the depredations of the invaders to a practical standstill by concentrating the population in their vast forests, where the enemy could not come, and where vegetable food was to be had in plenty by merely reaching out and plucking it from the luxuriant growths. They were now turning their attention to furnishing food and other assistance to Earth and Mars, and this was the first cargo of food from Venus— Jupiter ships being occupied in supplying foodstuffs to Mars.

The *"Therma"* had reported from the time of leaving Venus that the elementals were circling above her in unusual numbers and finally in dense clouds. A message came through, then, that they were drawing in closer as if to attack her. No great alarm was felt however, as the large ships had not been molested, and in any event it was felt there could be no danger. The *"Therma"* was 2,417 feet in length, nearly 600 feet in central diameter, and one of the most powerful etherships in existence.

The next message ran:

"The elementals are alighting on the ship. At first there were only a few, as if they were testing us out to see what we would do, but now they number many thousands, and the portholes are covered with them so that we have no means of telling what is happening outside. It is difficult to see how they can do us any harm. The passengers are calm and there is more curiosity than fear among them. They are going about the usual routine of occupations and amusements. In the main salons they are dancing, listening to concerts and radio news as usual. We are about 11,500,000 miles from Venus. Will reach Earth this evening or tomorrow."

There was an hour or two of silence and then the *"Therma"* operator came through again.

"Our navigators report that the *"Therma"* is showing a marked deviation from course, which they have not, as yet been able to correct. This is causing considerable wonder, and, naturally, some concern. It has been kept from the passengers so far. It may be well to warn other ships."

Another silence, then:

"The navigators report that present course would, if maintained, carry us directly toward The Outside, without approaching any planet. Someone has leaked the information and now all the passengers know. There is much alarm, but so far no panic. They are behaving wonderfully, particularly considering we are completely blanketed with these beastly creatures and going blindly and helplessly toward unknown space. Advise all ethergoing ships to make nearest ports at once."

The reports grew steadily fainter, and after many days ceased altogether. There was an apparent attempt to give their distance, but this could not be made out. The last words came in scattering and faint:

"—believe—lost—our—friends. Warn—"

It was the end of the gigantic *"Therma"* and her thousands of human souls.

In the succeeding weeks vessels in ever-increasing numbers failed to reach port. Some of them sent out their last brave, pitiful messages to the human race while on the way to meet an unknown doom; some merely dropped out of sight without a sound. The ships that were fortunate enough to reach port remained there. It was the end of ether navigation. Steps had to be taken to protect the ethergoing ships from the elementals. But this meant a long delay while new and more powerful generators were being installed and the ships remodeled for electric protection. The question was whether the Earth could hold out until the great number of vessels necessary to supply anything like an adequate source of food, could be rebuilt and dispatched.

The elementals were closing in on their prey. One by one they were cleverly cutting off the last supports of their beleaguered victims. Concurrently it began to be reported that they were drawing gradually away from Venus and Jupiter, and concentrating their attention on Earth and Mars, now entirely cut off from the other planets except for communication.

It was just about the end of the second year of the siege, and the height of the new mental bedlam and the disasters to interplanetary shipping, that Ello-ta, assisted by the brilliant Sanderson, and at all times under the immediate and active supervision and counsel of Mansonby, succeeded, after innumerable disheartening failures, in completing the construction of his first super-telepath.

AT the moment Mansonby, Ello-ta, and Sanderson were alone in the big room where the complicated machinery was installed. Painstakingly they were going over every smallest detail of the assembly once more. The crisis was at hand. And it was a crisis. Would this delicate, intricate thing of man's making do what it was to be commanded to do? Everything else had been tried—and everything else had failed. Would this last hope fail also? If it did fail, what was to become of the planets Mars and Earth and their people? It was a thing to whisper about. In spite of all the calm and scientific poise of these men, there was an intensity that could not be denied or put away. It is not easy to keep the blood cool and the heart calm when the next turn of the hand is going to spell salvation or unspeakable defeat for oneself; and above all for one's dear ones, and for one's own planet and perhaps all the other planets of a great solar system. For these men the world stood still. The doings of its countless centuries seemed focused and centered in that one room— standing still, waiting and watching what these men were doing. The world had done its utmost in its own defense and had failed. It now stood face to face—with the end.

Would this mechanism of theirs save them, or would it turn and rend them? Would this mental juggernaut they had made crush them under its mental wheels? Would it set in motion forces so gigantic that once started they could not be halted?

In the minds of these men at that tense moment must have been the image of a desolate Earth given over to utter calamity and desolation, its brave men, and its beautiful women, and all its sweet babes gone to return never more, and the good, kind old parent Earth, that had borne them so faithfully, strangled and dead beneath the foul, slimy embrace of the hideous serpent-octopi of an unknown hell.

A little nervously, as if putting off the last act, the three went over the assembly one more time. Every part seemed to be in place and adjustment. Well, the curtain must be raised. They must play out the last act of the drama to the end.

Mansonby nodded to Ello-ta, and the Cerean reached out and closed a switch—merely moved a little piece of metal a fraction of an inch, so that it would make contact with two other little pieces of metal and close a circuit that had stood open. It hardly seemed that this brief movement of the hand could be the one that was to deliver to the world its salvation or its destruction. At the same time that Ello-ta closed the switch, the other two men manipulated certain adjustments of a series of seven immense glass tubes. Eight feet high they stood, these tubes, small at the ends and expanding at the middle like a Coolidge tube.

Perhaps the gods of the machine assumed a bit more of nonchalance than they felt. Perhaps they failed to look into each other's eyes, pretending that there might be some small detail that requited them to look elsewhere.

"Ah-h-h!" The single syllable escaped from one of them in a whisper that could hardly be heard. The first of the great tubes had begun to show a dim phosphorescent glow. Slowly, as their eyes held upon it, fascinated, the glow deepened—slowly—how slowly! "Ah-h-h." The second tube of the series began to glow also; deepened. The third; the fourth; at last the entire series of seven were quivering with an unearthly, weird, ghostly light, or, was it a shadow—a shadow of something that could not be?

The Cerean closed another switch, and a low humming set in that seemed to put every molecule of the air into intense vibration. It deepened. Deeper still! So profound it became that the air seemed to whisper eerily of presences, of—things that men cannot give a name to—a quality of electric tenseness and strain that was in some vague way disturbing—distressing. It seemed as if the hand of a giant ghost were grasping the brain and twisting it—painfully. The eyes of the three men met for an instant—and then their glances turned aside.

Pausing to see that all parts of the complex creation were functioning properly, the Cerean, with a gesture of finality, entered a small soundproof and vibration-proof cabinet in the very center of the assembly. He moved resolutely now. Placing himself at an ordinary small telepath device, which fed into the assembly, he meticulously adjusted a helmet-like affair upon his head. Sanderson and Mansonby stood quietly to one side and waited, watching critically. The final crucial test was under way now. The fruit of their long labors was to be plucked for the worlds, or else—turn ashes on the winds of despair.

On the floor above, Martin, at his desk, writing, paused

*The first of the great tubes had begun to show a dim, phosphorescent glow. Slowly, as their eyes held upon it, fascinated, the glow deepened. The second tube of the series began to glow also; deepened. The third; the fourth...*

sharply in the middle of a word, and held his pen poised above the last character. He tried to go on, but in a moment laid the pen down and straightened in his chair. He pressed himself back tightly into it, gripped an arm with one hand, while the other brushed his brow. It seemed as if he were resisting—steeling himself against some overpowering impulse—or suggestion. Some seconds he sat thus, his face a medley of indecipherable emotions. Then his hands loosened and slid powerlessly from the arms of the chair; he leaned forward a little, his, face drawn, as if with suffering. Slowly, as if in spite of his utmost effort, he arose, and went toward the door; opened it and went out into a hallway. Ellis was just ahead of him, and there were others about, too—a Hindu, a Japanese, a man from Mercury. Some were going toward the escalators that led to the floor below; some were headed for the stairways; others were at the elevators. When they reached the next floor a number of others were before them, going in the direction of the door of the room where the gods of the machine waited. Others were coming up from floors below the 249th—by the escalators, elevators, stairways. It seemed as if the entire human content of the building was doing the one thing it had the power to do—being suddenly drawn by some mysterious, irresistible mental magnet to one point—the door that led into that one room. It was as if they all were caught in the grip of an overpowering current that was dragging them, whether they would go or would not.

Nobody paid much attention to anybody else. In all their mental world there was room for but the one thought—to go to the room where the seven tubes glowed, and the air was charged to shattering tension; where the three men waited, the Cerean in the cabinet with the helmet-like affair on his head, thrusting every atom of his plant mentality into the little telepath, in front of him that fed into the assembly.

As the room began to fill, Mansonby disconnected the switch, and Ello-ta emerged from the cabinet to look his company over with a languid half-smile—little as if the greatest thing the world had ever dreamed had just been done.

"Thanks for coming," he said, "but—to what, do we owe this pleasure?"

The company looked at each other and about, with a puzzled questioning air, and at first no one answered. Mansonby and Martin were standing beside Sanderson and Ello-ta, smiling in a knowing way. Adrienne, Mary Terra, Therma Lawrence, and Sigma Latourelle, with another young woman, entered softly on tiptoe from a side room and stood back of them—their faces a little white and showing the devastating strain.

At length a distinguished-looking young woman spoke. It was none other than the brilliant, rapier-minded scientist, Professor Melba Kasson—the same who had accompanied the expedition to Jupiter for the rescue of the Cereans from the clutches of the Drugos of the Hot Lands. She had joined Mansonby's forces shortly after the return. She looked from Sanderson to Ello-ta, and her eyes came to rest on Mansonby.

"You wished—you sent for me? Or did you?—no." One hand brushed her forehead. "I believe that I—had an appointment. To tell the truth, I'm—a little confused. Why are all these others here? I can't tell for the life of me what I did come about; but I suddenly remembered I was to come here—at once." She broke off sharply, with a gesture of annoyed bewilderment. "Chief, I discharge myself. I'm slipping. When a person forgets—"

Mansonby smiled at her. "Sit down, Professor, and wait a minute. You're all right." He turned to Ello-ta. "All right, Zah, you may reverse your procession."

Again the complicated mechanism was placed in operation; the tubes glowed and deepened; the air became electrically strained and tense. Ello-ta returned to the cabinet, resumed the helmet-like affair and there was silence. Someone put a hand suddenly to his head, as if there were a hurt there; there was a sort of choking gasp from another. "Oh!" exclaimed a woman in a frightened little voice, her hand at her throat. Then, without further ado—without preface or apology, rather as if it were the one most urgent and necessary thing on Earth at that precise moment, one after another they began to hasten out. All had gone out except the inner circle of the knowing ones, and the door had closed.

The machine ceased and Ello-ta emerged from the cabinet and stood before them. "Well?"

Mansonby offered one hand to the Cerean and the other to Sanderson. "Perfect! My hearty congratulations." The silence that followed was almost an awed one. Professor Kasson was the first to break it. "I begin to see why I couldn't remember. I—why, it's a miracle. It's a plain miracle and nothing else."

"You withdraw your discharge, I hope, Professor Kasson?" smiled the Chief in the way that made the worlds love him.

"With pleasure, Chief. I thought I was—slipping, or—"

## CHAPTER NINE

THE enormity of the thing had stunned everybody's nerves. There were staccato exclamations, with odd little silences between; peculiar sounds that suggested reconsidered beginnings of speech; a disinclination to do anything but stand and stare at the thing of steel, and glass, and fibers that Man had made and put brains into.

Mansonby was the first to pull himself together.

"You might explain a little, Zah, for the benefit of some of these. Is it a telepath?"

"Of course it is that; but it is more." The Cerean made a lazy gesture. "Much more. It is a telepath, because it assists in sending and receiving thought. But in that particular it is only a little more efficient, perhaps, than the small ones long in operation. As you know, the telepath is still an imperfect reader of thought; does not enable one to translate all thought. Neither does this. It is as dependent as ever upon mental pictures or images, the interpretation of which must be served with some ingenuity, but they are sent and received with so great force as to be practically irresistible. As you have seen, I used it to call you all here. I did that by merely sending you a picture of this room, coupled with its number in the building; and the picture was impressed with such force upon your brains that they supplied the impulse to come here—commanded your muscles to bring you here. You would have fought or killed to get here."

He paused as if to order his thoughts. "Thought-reading is not the purpose of this." He gestured toward the complex assembly, between which and the speaker's face all eyes wavered continually, and went on in a changed tone. "I neither hope, nor should I care, to read the minds of the elementals. I doubt if it is possible, although they have shown they possess mentality—very powerful mentality. Doubtless their mental processes would be starkly unintelligible to us."

"Then I'm puzzled as to its exact purpose, Mr. Ello-ta," said the young woman scientist.

"I'll try to explain. You know that the old telepath, in addition to mental pictures, reproduced moods. If the thinker who is being received is in a mood of despair, fear, happiness, one of those moods is impressed upon the receiving person—or mind. That you all know."

There were some nods and the Cerean went on.

"This mechanism is meant primarily to deal with those moods—to impress fear—and other moods, but chiefly fear, for our present purposes. Its power is so great that if I turned it upon the people and sent out the suggestion of fear, they would probably go into an insane frenzy—perhaps some would die of fright. That is because the mechanism gigantically intensifies or magnifies, whatever word you like to use, the force of the thought-waves until they become a dynamic, driving, irresistible vortex of force—a terrific blast of thought-force. It becomes more than what we usually think of as thoughts, or thought; it is a physical power. This machine puts its sensitive but powerful finger on the place of the union or interaction of thought and matter, and applies the most powerful force existing directly to matter. To illustrate: A man with a powerful mind and weak muscles can lift only what his muscles are equal to. No matter how powerful his will, if his muscles are atrophied or paralyzed he can lift nothing at all. Will and muscle—mind and matter— must co-ordinate to achieve results. This machine supplies both. The thought power we have always had, but we have not before been able to achieve the mental muscles for it to act upon.

"Here is a point: It works *on all mind.* Note I do not say *minds,* but *mind.* You know *mind* is *mind,* whether manifested in a man, a dog, an insect, or—an elemental. Mind is the primordial essence. There are not two *kinds* of *mind,* but only degrees of manifestation and strength. This would affect a herd of cattle or sheep, a flock of birds, or a swarm of bees, just the same as a gathering of human beings."

"Ah! I begin to see!" exclaimed Professor Kasson, her keen, intelligent face brightening.

"Exactly. Now another thing we had to work out: this machine can broadcast in concentric waves in all directions, like ripples on a pool; or it can be focused and sent out in any desired direction. Also, it can be set to affect any particular person, the length of whose thought-wave is known, or it can, as I have said, be made general, to affect all wavelengths. But what you see here is only a small part—only one unit, which has been set up for a preliminary test. Other units can and will be added in series, like the units of a voltaic pile, until the force is incalculable—cataclysmic. It will be the basic force of all forces, incalculably magnified in power. A piece of steel, a stone, or a board cannot move itself, any more than a man's muscle or body, until this omnipotent thought force is applied to it in some way."

Melba Kasson's keen eyes remained upon Ello-ta expectantly, and as he started to turn away, clearly deeming the explanation sufficient, she put out a detaining hand. There was no indirection or pretense about this able girl. What she was, she was, straight from the shoulder, without any thought for consequences or appearances.

"All right, Mr. Ello-ta, but wait, won't you?" she pleaded, with a short little laugh. "I see somebody has to perform the duty of being stupid, and it might as well be me as someone else. Your explanation is very clear as to the general principles—very general. You've made it clear that the basic force in the universe is thought—whatever that may be; that it controls matter absolutely—whatever matter may be—and is the only thing that does or can control matter; that you first amplify that power, then direct or focus it, then drive it out as a terrific force to act on anything else that itself has thought-power. *But*—"

The girl chanced to turn to Mansonby. On his face was mirrored a number of emotions. "My dear Professor Kasson," he said, smiling broadly at her, "I could love you for that. Once more like that and the Interplanetary will be compelled to at least double your already sizable compensation. Thanks for relieving me of being the goat. Someday somebody is going to suspect that I don't know any more than the rest do." He swung round to the Cerean, but the girl stopped him with a laugh.

"Please, Mr. Mansonby—I'll do the job to the end now. Remember you're supposed to know everything. Now, Mr. Ello-ta, as I was about to say, in behalf of people like Mr. Mansonby and myself—you've told us your device does certain remarkable things. How does it do them? How? Extraordinary as this assembled mass of apparatus is, it is still only dead matter. There isn't a speck of anything in it but dead matter; there isn't a speck of *life* in it. And yet it looks to people like Mr. Mansonby and myself, as if instead of mind controlling matter, this thing here takes hold of mind and controls it to its purpose. Please clear up a few points of the how."

Ello-ta gave a gesture of comic despair. "Now, Professor, why did you do that? I knew somebody would, but I thought I was through without it. However, since the damage is done, I'll have to crawl through as best I can. First, I may as well say now, since it would probably be found out later, anyway—there are many things I don't myself understand completely. The great mystery of the precise manner of interaction of mind and matter may never be made entirely clear. First, your point about the machine being a dead thing. So it is. But so, too, is everything else that the mind uses as a tool in executing its orders. You speak into a simple amplifier, which is nothing but an aggregation of dead parts; and yet immediately your voice is made many times more powerful. Substitute a microphone for the simple amplifier, and add a few other dead parts, and your voice is at once able to carry to a distant planet. Yet take away the voice—the mind behind the voice, let us say—the mind that wills to force the air through your vocal chords—themselves dead matter—and there is nothing left but deadparts—helpless parts."

He paused a moment to order his thoughts.

"Now, here, Professor Kasson: Why have we used women for this task? Because the female mind possesses a certain acuteness or intensity—a certain electromotive force, may I say?—that the masculine mind lacks. And why do we *train* them?"

"And how?" softly put in Professor Kasson, who was hanging on every word with bright eyes and bated breath.

Ello-ta nodded acknowledgement of the question. "Answering first the question. Why do we train them? To enable them to employ the utmost of their mental power. It is well known that normally the human being employs only a relatively small part of his potential mental force. This training is a matter of voluntary, sustained effort—experience. Answering your question. How do we train them? First, by placing their brains under the influence of a powerful electro-mental stimulating field of force, which wakens and vitalizes the dormant mental forces and makes them dynamic. That's the best I can give you on that at the moment, Professor. Then this awakened, stimulated, vitalized, and experienced force is turned through this ordinary simple telepath, which gives it coherence and body, directiveness—*focus.*"

"That's clear." It was Mansonby speaking. "Now this…" He waved toward the super-machine.

"Yes. Right there is where this steps in—or, rather, where we step into it. We have now the mind forces of our 50 odd operators at their top notch of efficiency. They are now no longer the more or less aimless, half-dormant things, like the ordinary run of mentalities under no stress or pressure. They are at their highest possible potential. *Now,* we hook the 50 odd telepaths into the first unit of our assembly, as you have seen here. What does it do? This unit does no more than to give this aroused and powerful, coherent and focused mass of mental force a vehicle to travel on. It gives it amperage, or intensity, and electromotive, or driving force, exactly as an ordinary electric potential is increased by the proper means from a weak and inefficient force to one of devastating power."

He gave a dismissive wave of the hand. "That's all—all. The successive units that will be placed in circuit merely add more power—that's all. You have only to remember, then, that these unpleasant beings—" he gestured to the mass of sinister beings floating overhead "—are less physical than we, and more mental; that their physicality is almost nil, and their mentality vastly ascendant."

"That does not mean," Mansonby explained, "that these elementals are more intelligent than we are. Don't get the wrong idea there. What Mr. Ello-ta is saying is that the elementals are made of a more tenuous and sensitive substance, or, to quote Professor Sanderson here, 'the mental or spiritual *element* is highly ascendant over the physical'."

Ello-ta nodded. "Thanks. All that remains to say then is that when at dawn tomorrow the things I have been talking about are put in train, and our operatives concentrate on the emotion of fear, fear, *fear,* terror, terror, *terror,* there will drive into the midst of these elementals, permeating and possessing and dominating their *mind*—note I do not say *minds*—a blasting force of fear and terror that will, we hope, sweep them from our skies back to the hells they came from."

When the explanation was over and the company had left, Ello-ta and Sanderson, with the assistance of expert technicians, began preparations for the assembling and connecting in series of five other sets, each the same as the first. It had proven itself. They knew what it would do. What remained was only the putting together.

Meantime, the trained women prepared themselves for their end of the task by super-charging their special potentials. At each of a hundred telepaths one of these super-sensitive ones would seat herself, bend her powers into it to the limit of human endurance. The preparation, under the charge of Hindu Adepts, would require all of the time until the assemblies were set up and made ready. Then this united current of thought power would surge into the first unit and through the series, magnifying as it shot through, and be focused upon the objective that hovered above them.

At last all was done and all were ready, awaiting only the hour before dawn. The mechanics had gone; the gods of the machine were snatching a few hours of rest before the supreme hour. One only could find no steep or rest—or peace in her heart. Silently she arose from her bed and went up the special stairway to the room where waited the machine of the gods. She knew the machine well; knew every nerve and fiber and muscle of the thing, having watched when no one suspected; knew its every adjustment and part. Deftly she threw the switch, manipulated the adjustments, prepared all things, and then set herself, white-faced and grim, at the telepath that thrust into the series of units. This was her supreme moment, that would mean for her the happiness of the only heaven possible for her, or—the agony of a ceaseless Gethsemane, while life lasted. Whether the elementals went or stayed would mean not the snap of a finger to her if she failed now. She had never given up; she had always felt that she *knew;* but, Ah, God! She could not know—she could not *know.*

But now she would know.

A few moments she paused to gather her forces, the helmet-like affair resting snugly over the auburn crown above her brown eyes. Then slowly, steadily, as she had been taught—not violently or spasmodically or hysterically—gradually drawing into a fierce, savage mental cry, the dial set to the wave length she knew so well, she cast her whole sublime woman's soul from her body and out into space. For her this one thing only existed in all the vast universe that God had made. What were a few mere universes compared to this one that she desired now?

An hour passed—another hour—and the girl had not moved so much as a hail's breadth, shut up in the little cabinet, which was to be her heaven or hell. Of time she knew nothing.

Of one thing only she knew.

With a savage, fierce intensity to which man is a stranger, and which is the nearest to God of anything he has made, she sat at her task.

And then—she knew! She knew! It was done. Wildly she cast the helmet from her head, dashed from the cabinet, and into the hallway. How woman knows, man cannot tell. Near the door of the machine gods' room she waited. Was—was that a sound? No! Yes! Yes, it was!

In that supreme moment she did not wait for slow mortal eyes.

"Cyrus! My dear one!" her soul breathed forth.

And, "Little one! Little one!" came back the clear reply.

THEN he came. Not the Marlin she had known, but a figure bedraggled and swaying, bearded, unkept, and unkempt. But the woman, as ever with woman, saw only the soul of the man. Before he could take another step she had leaped for his arms. Without a word they clung together. After a while she led him back into the room of the gods of the machine, and sat him down and crept into his still powerful arms, and lay there quietly, happily, her face against his.

She remembered she had not turned off the machine. She did it now and hurried back to the heavenly arms. At last she spoke. "You have been in terrible trouble, Cyrus, my dear. I know you would have come if you could, but—"

"Where have I been, little one? Why, let me see... I had to do something for the—the Chief." He was startled. "The Chief! The Chief! Is he—?"

"He is all right, dear," she soothed him, and he relapsed again.

"I went to—St.—"

"Yes, St. Louis, dear," she prompted.

"St. Louis, yes, and then to—" there had been an accident—he could not remember from that point on—anything—except—Yes! His car had been wrecked! He seemed to recall dimly wandering, wandering, always wandering through the months, looking for something he could not find, or even remember. And then he had seemed to awaken as from some strange trance and found that he was in New York, and he had felt the irresistible call to go to that place.

"Never mind, dear, never mind. Don't try to remember—now. It will all come back to you. Don't try now. My dear one—my dear!"

A sound suddenly snatched her back to sterner realities, then, and she started up from the heavenly arms. "Cyrus! The dawn! It is nearly dawn!" She glanced at the brightening light through the windows. "They are coming at the dawn to make the supreme test of the machine here. Someone is coming now." She put aside his puzzled inquiries about the strange machine. "No—not now, beloved. I will explain it all later. I must fix you up before they see you, and be ready to take my place with the others. Come to my room. We must hurry. There is little time. I forgot. Come."

She took him by the hand and the big man went obediently.

They were hardly gone when the operatives and others began to arrive, and soon, with drawn faces and tensed souls these magnificent women—Adrienne Ello-ta and Therma Lawrence, the little Jovian Mary Terra, Narsatta No-tonta, the Martian, and the others, all picked with deliberate care for this supreme moment—were taking up their stations in the separate little sound-proof and vibration-proof cabinets.

Great Man was making his last grim stand against the gruesome fields of the primordial hell-pits.

When the Father Sun looked above the great waters, the people awoke to their salvation. In all the sunlit firmament there was not a lingering sign of the detestable enemy.

At the close of a day Mary Terra took Cyrus by the hand, now pretty much himself again, and they went out and strolled by the rainbowed fountains of an evening that was sweet of grass and flowers, and the city—and the whole regenerated Earth—was immersed in fragrant peace.

## THE END